P. M. Hubbard and The

>>> This title is part of The Murder Room, our series dedicated to making available out-of-print or hard-to-find titles by classic crime writers.

Crime fiction has always held up a mirror to society. The Victorians were fascinated by sensational murder and the emerging science of detection; now we are obsessed with the forensic detail of violent death. And no other genre has so captivated and enthralled readers.

Vast troves of classic crime writing have for a long time been unavailable to all but the most dedicated frequenters of second-hand bookshops. The advent of digital publishing means that we are now able to bring you the backlists of a huge range of titles by classic and contemporary crime writers, some of which have been out of print for decades.

From the genteel amateur private eyes of the Golden Age and the femmes fatales of pulp fiction, to the morally ambiguous hard-boiled detectives of mid twentieth-century America and their descendants who walk our twenty-first century streets, The Murder Room has it all. >>>

The Murder Room
Where Criminal Minds Meet

themurderroom.com

P. M. Hubbard (1910–1980)

Praised by critics for his clean prose style, characterization, and the strong sense of place in his novels, Philip Maitland Hubbard was born in Reading, in Berkshire and brought up in Guernsey, in the Channel Islands. He was educated at Oxford, where he won the Newdigate Prize for English verse in 1933. From 1934 until its disbandment in 1947 he served with the Indian Civil service. On his return to England he worked for the British Council, eventually retiring to work as a freelance writer. He contributed to a number of publications, including *Punch*, and wrote 16 novels for adults as well as two children's books. He lived in Dorset and Scotland, and many of his novels draw on his interest in and knowledge of rural pursuits and folk religion.

Flush as May
Picture of Millie
A Hive of Glass
The Holm Oaks
The Tower
The Custom of the Country
Cold Waters
High Tide
The Dancing Man
A Whisper in the Glen
A Rooted Sorrow
A Thirsty Evil
The Graveyard
The Causeway
The Quiet River
Kill Claudio

A Hive of Glass

P. M. Hubbard

An Orion book

Copyright © Caroline Dumonteil, Owain Rhys Phillips and Maria Marcela Appleby Gomez 1965, 2012

The right of P. M. Hubbard to be identified as the author of this work has been asserted in accordance with the Copyright, Designs and Patents Act 1988.

This edition published by
The Orion Publishing Group Ltd
Orion House
5 Upper St Martin's Lane
London WC2H 9EA

An Hachette UK company
A CIP catalogue record for this book is available from the British Library

ISBN 978 1 4719 0073 0

www.orionbooks.co.uk

Printed and bound by CPI Group UK Ltd, Croydon, CR0 4Y

With gratitude to
CECIL DAVIS LTD
of Grosvenor Street,
who on the 24th June, 1963, at Sotheby's,
paid £6,500 for the K.Y. Goblet by Verzelini,
but are still ready to help the small collector

1

The paint was going, but you could just about read it. It said 'Furniture & Antiques'. My foot eased on the accelerator as a simple reflex. You never know, especially with these dingy little places. The big towns and the tourist places are hopeless. Practically nothing there, and speculative prices for what there is, well over honest London rates. But this was a third-class manufacturing town, and the shop was pure junk in an outlying street.

I put the car round a left-hand corner in a small brick sidestreet of unrelieved ugliness. I got out and put on an old macintosh. My speech was undisguisably southern, but at least I did not look like a visitor. I might be in any sort of business.

I walked back past a window loaded with every sort of small stuff. I felt slightly sick, and knew that there was a vein throbbing on the right side of my temple. It is an odd business, this collector's passion. I have not read the psychologists on the subject, but I have no doubt it is a substitute for some more honest emotion. Not sex, I think. More likely the hunting instinct, or something from the food-gathering mesolithic. It is certainly a disease of civilisation, and most civilisations formalise sex rather than overlay it.

Also, although I know it is easy for one collector to deride another, it surely makes some difference what you collect. I may be a bit silly at times, but the man who would do murder for a cigarette card is obviously a case. I turned back, opened the door and went in.

The door rang an electric bell—this was not the industrial

Midlands for nothing—but there was no one there. It was cluttered almost to the ceiling. I ignored the furniture and brass, the rolled-up carpets and the folded stacks of dead men's blankets. I peered through them, but there was nothing behind them. I made for the shelves at the back of the shop. There was some china, one bit probably worth looking at for anyone interested in china, and behind it three rows of dusty glass.

The man appeared suddenly from behind a mahogany wardrobe. There must have been a door in the side wall. He was a bit withered, but not seedy. He would probably have a pension of sorts, and junk was only a side-line. He had the Midlander's expression of anticipated outrage. I said, 'Good morning, sorry to bother you,' because I felt he expected an apology for my coming in at all. He grunted, but his suspicion was unallayed.

I said, 'I wondered if there was anything one could put flowers in. Something small. Niece of mine likes old bits.'

He dragged his eyes away from mine reluctantly, as if he did not know what I might be looking at unless he held them. He looked disparagingly round the shop.

'I don't know,' he said. 'Sort of a vase?'

'Yes, or an old jug, or a mug or something. Even an old glass. I don't want anything big.'

He said, 'Seen anything in the window?' He still wanted to know why I had come in at all.

'I didn't look properly. Might be something.' I picked up an Edwardian milk jug and turned it round in my hands, daring him to go to the window and leave me unwatched. He hesitated and then went. He moved a table and a couple of folding picture frames collapsed in a small cloud of dust. He muttered and stooped to pick them up. I was already at the shelf of glass, looking behind the chipped jugs and the uncouth moulded tumblers. My mouth was dry.

There is no mistaking the gleam of eighteenth-century

2

glass. I still think it is a passion you need not be ashamed of, unless you let it get out of hand. It is a characteristic product of the ultimate flowering of our civilisation, before industrialisation brought wealth and mechanisation, and they started to carbonado even a good quality glass till it looked like cheap paste. There was just that hundred years or so, between the time they learnt to change the composition of George Ravenscroft's glass so that it did not crizzle and the time they abandoned the natural magic of the centrifuge for the artificial glitter of the sharp edge. Just that time when they could not put a hand wrong, whether it was a tavern ale glass or a tall beauty to contain the ebullience of the wild early champagnes. Thousands and thousands of beautiful drinking glasses, all broken and buried now except for the odd ones that remain to shame and tantalise us. All what they call collectors' pieces, and fewer and fewer of them anywhere but in the collections.

I heard him coming back from the window and turned to meet him with an expression of mild interest. He had a pewter beer mug and a piece of Birmingham brass. 'There's these,' he said.

I took the beer mug and looked at it with interest. I said, 'That might do. A bit big, really, for what I want.' I put it down on a small clear space of dusty table top. I put the flowery china jug beside it. Then I turned to the glass shelf and took down the horrible tumbler from the front row. I could see more clearly now what stood behind it in the back row. I gave an amused grunt and lifted it out, trying to make my hand look careless. 'That's a funny one,' I said. My voice sounded wildly unnatural. It was an utterly filthy, quite faultless Newcastle light baluster, all of ten inches high, the rounded perfect bowl perched on a breathless series of knops. I said, 'I wonder where that came from?'

He looked at me pretty sharply. He did not know a thing, but like all his kind he was a natural businessman, and something of my excitement got through to him. He said, 'That'd be an old glass. Don't see many like that.'

He took it from me and dusted it roughly with a slightly oily piece of rag. My hand went after the glass, but I controlled it. I watched it in his hands, licking my lips. At last he put it down on the table with the other two. It was cleaner now. Surely no one could miss the quality of it.

I said, 'Quaint, though, isn't it?' I still sounded mildly amused. He did not say anything. He never stopped looking at me.

I looked at the three of them sitting there, the solid inoffensive mug, the dreadful jug and the utterly perfect glass. I picked up the jug, looked at it all over and put it back on the shelf. I said, 'Suppose I take those two?'

He looked from me to the glass and back again. His common sense was battling with his dreadful businessman's instinct, which told him something was up. He said, 'That'd be ten bob for the mug.'

I said, 'What—' My throat was completely dry and my voice stuck. I coughed and said, 'What about the glass, then?'

He said again, 'That'd be an old glass.' He looked at me and took the plunge. 'I'd have to charge you—' His voice stopped, and I could see a wheel turning in his head, clocking up figure after figure, while he tried to make up his mind where to stop it. He said, '—three pounds for the glass.'

This was the moment. I whistled and looked at him quizzically. I said, 'That's a bit steep, isn't it? Not all that special, is it?' Relief flooded into his eyes. He had been afraid I would jump at it. He said again, 'It's an old glass, that.'

I said, 'I rather like it, but three quid's a bit steep, surely?' He did not say anything, and I pretended to consider the matter. I said, 'Let's see—' I took out my wallet and looked

4

in it as if I was not sure what I had got and what I could spare. He still did not say anything.

I took out four pound notes and held them out to him. He was in a rage of uncertainty again, but he could not help taking them in his hand. I picked up the mug in my left hand, and the glass, very carefully, in my right. We stood and looked at each other. I said, 'If you can find me ten bob.' My voice was hoarse now, and his eyes were aflame with resentment. He stood there, holding the notes in his hand. Then he held out his other hand and said, 'Don't you want it wrapped?' He said it, not them.

I shook my head, put my hands carefully in front of me and pushed past him to the door of the shop. He said, 'Here—' Then he came after me. 'I've changed my mind,' he said. 'I'm not selling.'

I said, 'You have sold.'

He put his two hands out, one holding the notes and the other reaching for the glass.

I said again, 'You have sold. You named a price. I accepted it and paid you. You've got the money. I've got the glass. The deal's complete. You can't go back on it now.'

He said, 'How do I know what it's worth? Worth a mint of money, some of them old ones.'

'This one's worth three quid,' I said. 'That's its market price. I've just bought it for that. What do you think I'm going to do? Sell it again and make a profit?'

He suddenly reached out as if to grab me—me, standing there with that beautiful fragile thing unprotected in my hand. I felt choked with rage at his ignorance and blind greed, and my left hand swung the heavy pewter mug up backhanded between his head and mine. He must still have been watching my eyes, because what he saw there set him back on his heels and he took his hand away quick.

I was still breathless with rage, but the moment of pressure had passed. I was under control again. I said, 'Are you going to call a policeman or am I? He'll tell you the same. I've bought it and paid for it, and it's mine.'

The pewter mug clanked on the brass door handle as I opened the door left-handed. He came out after me, but keeping his distance. 'It's a bloody swindle,' he said. 'That's what it is, a bloody swindle.'

I said, 'Tell that to the police.' I walked off along the pavement swinging the mug and holding the glass close in front of me. He came a little way after me, changed his mind and darted back into the shop. I watched him in and then ran to the corner. There was no one in the sidestreet, and I went straight to the car. I wrapped the glass in successive sheets of *The Times*, bundling the paper well round that precious vulnerable stem. There was still no one about. I put the whole package carefully in the boot, got into the driving seat and waited, watching the mirror.

I had not been there fifteen seconds when he crossed the end of the street. He had two large young men with him. They hardly glanced at the back of the car as they went across. I did a copy-book three-pointer, drove back to the main street and turned right. As I passed the shop I saw one of their wives in the doorway, awaiting the warriors' return. She was a horror. She did not look at me.

I drove a couple of miles back the way I had come and turned off into the lanes. It was green, rather heavy country, never quite clear of the smell of the towns. The next turning might have been for Ambridge. I stopped and walked down through a field to a stream, carrying my package.

I knelt by the water, dropped *The Times* sheet by sheet behind me and washed the glass gingerly with my finger tips in the clear water, easing off the old grime and the taint of my vendor's oily rag. The thing came to life startlingly under my caressing fingers, and when at last I held it up, I fairly caught my breath.

6

The man said, 'What's it, then, something you've just found?'

'Bought,' I said. I recognised him at once. It was Jack Archer.

He nodded. 'Pretty,' he said. He really meant it. Your countryman is still essentially civilised. 'Worth a bit, is it?'

I said, 'Difficult to say now. Prices change so. Thirty quid, perhaps.'

He whistled appreciatively. 'What did you pay for it, then?'

'Three,' I said. 'No, three ten.' I never got my change.

He nodded cheerfully. 'Nice to pick up a thing like that. You a dealer?'

'Not me,' I said. 'This is for myself.'

'Ah, that's right. Glad you had it so cheap.' He nodded and went off soft-footed in the squelchy grass. I loved him as much as I had hated the man in the shop. I wrapped the glass up again, turning the clean side of the paper inwards, and went back to the car. I wanted to sing.

When I got home I washed it again in warm soft water and a mild detergent. Then I put it on a table by itself in the middle of the room and sat and looked at it. Then I got the books out.

This is one of the big moments. However much you think you know, there are always things you cannot carry in your head, or things you want confirmed. But above all you are, as it were, showing it to somebody for the first time, seeing whether your passionate conviction will stand up to the cold light of expert judgment. It is a frightening business, and hardly ever quite decisive, because no two glasses are ever quite alike. One man's description covers it, but is not quite comprehensive or explicit. Another has a picture of something very like it, but disagrees with the first man's date or origin. What you have got was made by a particular crafts-man at a particular place and time, and may have been one

7

of several dozen almost exactly similar. But now the name has gone, and the place and time are matters of inference and expert opinion: and all its companion pieces were long since smashed and thrown away. It is perfect in itself, this thing that has come into your hands after two hundred years of precarious existence, but you can never know the whole truth about it.

Finally I did what I always do. I filled it, after God knows how many years of drought and emptiness, with a good claret and drank it solemnly, wondering who had last drunk from it and what. Then I washed it and put it in its place.

As soon as he heard my voice on the phone, David groaned. He said, 'Oh God, what is it now? Can I bear it?'

I said, 'Newcastle. Nearly ten inches. A blade, then two drop knots, then a sort of baluster with tears, and a cushion over a high domed foot. No flaw.'

There was a pause, and he said, 'Say that again.' I told him again.

'Where the hell did you find that?'

'Junk shop.'

'Blast you,' he said, 'blast you. I'll come in tomorrow. All right?'

'All right.'

'Have you seen the July *Old Glass*?'

'No. It's here. I haven't looked at it yet. Why?'

'Levinson,' he said. 'Guess what.'

'Tell me.'

'A tazza by Verzelini. Dedicatory inscription. Out of this world.'

I said, 'There isn't one. They say he made them.'

David said, 'There is now. Levinson's got it. Dedicated to the Queen.'

'I don't believe it.'

'There are photos. And Levinson knows. Unless it's a hoax on his part.'

'Not Levinson,' I said.

'No—well, there you are. You'd better look at it.'

'I will,' I said. I rang off, pulled the magazine to me over the table and ripped off the cover. There was a headline right across the cover. It said, 'A Verzelini Tazza'.

2

Old Glass was one of the most beautifully produced quarterlies in the world. To anyone of civilised tastes it was a delight to look at, and even to handle. To the addict it combined this aesthetic perfection with something of the sanctity of holy writ, as a thing like the Luttrell Psalter must have done in a less sophisticated and more religious age. Not that *Old Glass* laid any claim to final authority. Its editorial line, so far as it had one, was confined to the less expert aspects of its subject. But its contributors were all men of authority, and it was the forum of choice for anyone who had anything to say about antique glass. It must have been over-contributed and under-subscribed.

The subscription was twenty guineas a year. The circulation was known only to Peter Sarrett, who owned it, edited it and apparently lived solely for it. But it must have run at a steady loss. It is dead now, and so is Peter. It ran for six years altogether, and the twenty-four numbers, especially a complete run, are already worth a great deal more than their original price. Peter was supposed to have a private income, and indeed must have. Wherever his money came from, it did not come from *Old Glass*. That was where it went.

I opened the July number—there was in fact only one more—at the astonishing first article. I was immediately struck by the comparative poverty of the illustrations, but the substance was breath-taking. For the sake of those who are not fellow addicts, I should perhaps say that Giacomo Verzelini was a Venetian who brought his city's knowledge and practice of glass-making to Elizabethan London, to the

10

disgust of the merchants who were importing glass from
Venice. It was a rough age, and their disgust took the practical form of burning down his works at the Savoy. Giacomo
appealed to his adopted sovereign, who could be as rough
as her subjects when she thought roughness was called for.
She granted Giacomo a twenty-year monopoly in the
making and selling of what she called 'Venice glasses'. The
merchants went out of business, but in that year, 1575, the
English glass industry really came into being, ready to
produce, two centuries later, some of the most wonderful
things ever made by man.

Compared with this later stuff, of course, Verzelini is a
primitive, but he is the great identifiable original. Every
remaining specimen is known and recorded, and to
announce a large piece with a dedicatory inscription to the
Queen was something on a par with announcing an un-
recorded Leonardo, signed by the master and dedicated in
his own hand to his patron. Of course, the public interest,
and the probable scale of cash values, was vastly less. But
to the connoisseur the thing was pretty electrifying, and to
anyone in the trade the money involved was dazzling.

A tazza, to be honest, is rather like a cake stand, or one
of those things (without the cover) they used to put ham
sandwiches on in railway buffets. It is a broad flat dish,
standing on a single central stem and foot. It had been
assumed, and generally stated, that Verzelini made them,
because anyone making glass then would have. No specimen had been known. And now here it was.

This brings me back to the illustrations. They were
respectable black and white photographs giving a reasonable definition, and would have been all right in a mass-
produced paper-back. For *Old Glass* they were wildly
inadequate. And there was something odd about the background. Nevertheless, they showed what was undeniably
a tazza of the right period. The top had been photographed

11

full-face to show the inscription. It was the thin, rather spidery diamond engraving of the time, and Giacomo, whether he was at home in English or not, had stuck to formal Latin.

Regae Alt^mae Elizabethae Adiutrici G^mo Verzelini d. dedicavit 1576.

Adiutrix was new to me, but it seemed acceptable, and, remembering the merchants, Giacomo was being no mere courtier in calling the Queen his helper.

As I say, it was all there. If the thing was what it looked in the pictures, and if Levinson was satisfied it was genuine, it was fabulous. Levinson's own report was curiously laconic. The tazza had come to hand, he did not say where from. He described its features and appearance, reproduced the inscription, commented on the *adiutrix* in relation to the date, and left it at that.

I got on the phone to Peter Sarrett. I knew that saturnine, dedicated man reasonably well, and I knew I should not be the only one. His number was in fact engaged, but I got him at last. I said, 'Peter, this Verzelini piece—'

Peter said, 'Who's that?'

'Sorry,' I said. 'Johnnie.'

'Oh, hullo, Johnnie. Yes?'

'This Verzelini piece of Levinson's—where did it come from?'

'I don't know.'

'Didn't you ask him?'

'I asked him, yes. He didn't say.'

'Is it his?'

'I don't know that, either. I tell you, I don't know where he found it, or where it is now, or who owns it. I only know what's in the article. I printed it on Levinson's authority. I thought it good enough.'

'You mean you haven't seen it?'

'No.'

12

'What about the photos?'

'Levinson's own.'

'That accounts for them. A bit amateur, aren't they? So what it comes to is that no one's seen the thing except Levinson?'

'So far as I know, no one.'

I whistled. He said, 'I'm afraid I'm not clear what's troubling you.'

'Nothing's troubling me. But it's an odd position, isn't it?'

'I don't see why. Levinson has chosen to publish like this, and of course I was glad to print it, though I'd have liked better pictures. But I spoke to him, naturally. The thing's genuine, if that's what you mean. Unless you doubt Levinson's authority. Or his good faith. I accept both.'

'Oh yes,' I said, 'of course. Well—thank you for telling me. I suppose we'll see it presently.'

'Yes. All right, Johnnie.' He rang off. I felt put down, but Peter was never an easy man to deal with.

David came round the next evening. He was a civil servant and busy, or at least engaged, during the day. I showed him my Tyneside beauty and gave him a slightly edited account of its rescue from the Midland junk shop. I had the beer mug on the mantelpiece as a sort of battle souvenir, and gestured with it dramatically.

David looked at me curiously. He said, 'You didn't actually hit him?'

'No, of course not. I'm not as potty as all that.'

He took the mug from me and weighed it in his hand. 'No,' he said, but he sounded uncertain.

I said, 'Anyway, wouldn't you have been pretty angry yourself?'

He ignored this. He said, 'I don't think you're potty, Johnnie, not by a long chalk. For a man of your age and solitary habit, I think you're still reasonably on the right

13

side of the line. All the same, I should avoid dramatic gestures with heavy beer mugs. That's all.' He laughed charmingly. David could be very charming.

I did not pursue the matter. I had my own very clear picture of the incident in the shop and I knew where I was with it. The thing I remembered most clearly was the way the man had dropped his hand and stood back, and that gave me pleasure rather than otherwise.

But the truth was that my Newcastle wine was over-shadowed in both our minds by Levinson's tazza. The fact that my anonymous Tyneside gaffer was a better craftsman than the old Venetian, and had two more centuries of tech-nical advance behind him, was neither here nor there. Nor was the fact that my glass was far more beautiful. To eighteenth-century eyes the Tudors were all barbarians, and in visual matters at least the eighteenth century was right. But to a collector, and in the cold light of Sotheby's sale room, there was no comparison. My glass was an ordinary collector's lucky strike. The tazza was, as I have said, fabulous.

I put the Newcastle wine on the centre table and said, 'Peter doesn't know where the thing is.'

'I know.'

'Did Peter tell you?'

'I rang him up. You too, I suppose. And at least a dozen other people. It took me some time to get on.'

'That may explain it,' I said. 'He was pretty offhand with me. I suppose he was sick of telling people. It's odd, though, isn't it?'

'I don't know. A bit, I suppose. But Levinson's a cagey old devil, and he genuinely hates a hullabaloo. He'd want to publish the find once he was sure of it, but he'd dodge the excitement if he could. I wonder what he means to do with it?'

'If it's his to do anything with,' I said.

'There's that, yes. If it's not—if it belongs to someone who isn't specially interested—it will come on the market, of course. No one who wasn't a pretty dedicated collector would sit on a thing like that.'

'What would it fetch, do you suppose?'

'God knows. The K.Y. Goblet fetched six and a half thousand in 1963, and this is in a different class. It can't be documented, I suppose, or we'd have heard of it sooner. But one must assume the Queen had it, and that alone would send it sky-high. I shouldn't think they'd let it go out of the country, anyway.' He picked up the Newcastle again, and looked at me. 'Suppose you'd found that instead of this in your junk shop. What would you have done?'

I laughed at him. 'Don't be silly,' I said. 'I wouldn't part with a thing like that if I was starving for a crust.'

'There you are,' he said. 'I told you. At least slightly potty. Not that I don't believe you.'

We looked at some of my others before David went. He had seen them all before, of course, but there is always something to say. One of my balusters, in particular, he wanted so badly that his handling of it had an almost masochistic touch. He was better off for light balusters than I was, and my new acquisition was less actively painful to him.

He said, 'Leave me that one in your will, Johnnie. You're a single man, and it would be terrible if it went for death duties. I'm ten years younger than you, and we married chaps always live longer.'

'That be damned,' I said. 'You wear yourselves out paying school bills. I'm living for years yet. But whatever happens to mine, it will stay together. God knows it's not much of a collection by some standards, but I'd like it to stay together.'

'Leave me the lot, then. They'd combine nicely with

mine.' He took himself off. It was still only a quarter past seven.

I got out the July *Old Glass* again and looked at Levinson's photos. I used my lens on them, but the detail was not there and it told me nothing. I was still puzzled by the background. It was not the dark, neutral background you would expect. There was something there, but it was blurred out, as if there had been some rather amateurish dodging done. I should like to have seen the negatives.

I dialled Levinson's number and asked if he was at home. A maid of some sort sounded doubtful, but presently Levinson came on the line. I said, 'Mr Levinson, this is Johnnie Slade speaking.'

'Oh yes. Good evening, Mr Slade.' Levinson's voice had a distinctive foreign quality. He was a distinguished old boy altogether. I supposed he was a Jew. I had no grounds for saying so really, but when a man is as civilised as that, and has a faint European accent and an anglicised name, one is always apt to assume it. He might, in fact, have come from anywhere in central Europe.

I said, 'I wonder if you could spare me a few minutes some time.'

He hesitated. I said, 'I wanted your opinion on a piece.' I did, in fact—not the Newcastle, which was straightforward enough.

He said, 'Oh yes?'

I laughed and said, 'If I promise not to mention the tazza—'

He did not laugh, but he spoke smiling. I knew that smile of his so well. 'Very well,' he said, 'of course. But I'll hold you to your promise, Mr Slade.'

'You can, really.'

'Good. Well, let me see. I have a guest for dinner, but I should be free by about half past ten. Is that too late for you?'

'No, indeed. It's very kind of you. I won't keep you long.'

'Good. I'll expect you, then. I hope you have something interesting.'

'So do I,' I said.

'Well, we'll see. I shall be alone. Just ring and come up. You know where to find me.' I thanked him and rang off.

I wrapped my glass in newspaper—your dealer uses tissue paper to impress the customer, but in fact newspaper is much more efficient—and put it in a cardboard box. It was quite a small one, a colour-twist I wanted to believe was English but had a feeling I should be told was Dutch. I walked to St John's Wood, which was where Levinson lived. It was a warm still night, with a suggestion of summer lightning unable to make itself seen through the London glare. There were not many people about, and those there were walked slowly. The women wore summer frocks with nothing over them.

I rang the front door bell and opened the door. It was a detached brick house, built somewhere in the late 'twenties and with a fringe of garden round it. It must have been worth an enormous amount of money, standing where it did. Levinson owned the whole house, but seemed to live almost entirely on the first floor. I thought I heard movement upstairs, but did not see anyone. I walked up the silent stairs, and as my head came level with the landing I picked up the strong, familiar smell of Levinson's cigar.

I opened the door of what for some reason he always called the library. It contained, in fact, a very complete set of reference books, two of them written by himself, but most of the walls were taken up with his show-cases. Levinson sat at his desk in the middle of the room, looking at me with his usual small, curiously sweet smile. A thin coil of smoke wound upwards from the cigar resting on the edge of

the ash-tray at his right hand. The whole room smelt of it.
His hands were in his lap.

I said, 'Good evening,' and then saw that something was
not quite right. I had moved, but his eyes had not. He was
warm, composed and friendly, but quite dead.

I cannot stand dead and broken things. I do not know
what started this, but it goes back a long way. It is not quite
the same as the fairly common thing about blood, though
blood makes it worse. It is the deadness. It seems odd when
I have a good deal of violence in me. Levinson, luckily, did
not look dead. There was nothing even to show why he had
died. There was nothing unnatural anywhere. There was
not even a particularly long ash on his cigar; but a good
cigar, left to itself, burns very slowly. I put my hand out to
the telephone and then stopped. Instead, I walked to the
door, opened it, put my head out and listened. There was
not a sound anywhere. I came back into the room.

It was not a particularly secretive room. There was no
safe or filing cabinet. His card indexes were on a side
table, under the bookshelf. Otherwise there was only the
desk. It was fairly well covered with papers, but did not
look untidy. It was the desk of a reasonably methodical
man who does plenty of paper work but keeps no secretary.
I put my hand out to the top left-hand drawer, took it back
and then, with the first consciously clandestine movement
I had made, wrapped my handkerchief round my fingers.

I do not know whether I really expected to find what I
did find. It was the tazza I was after, from that moment,
but I doubt if I had any conscious immediate purpose.
What I found in the third drawer on the left-hand side was
an envelope, unsealed, with the date 'June 12' written on
the front in pencil. It contained six negatives.

I held one up to the desk lamp, knowing, even before I
did so, that it would be one of his photos of the tazza. It was
a side view, tilted slightly, so that it showed the detail of the

18

stem under the broad top. I had been right in my suspicion
of the prints. The thing was held in two small thin hands. It
was held in such a way that the hands did not come between
the camera and any part of the glass. One was flat under
the foot and the other pressed with its finger tips at the
centre of the top.

Old Levinson, sitting there so quietly at his desk and not
looking at me, had used a dodger to black out, in the print,
everything but the glass. Why he had to go to those lengths
instead of simply sticking the thing on a table and photo-
graphing it I could not imagine. It was the same in all six
negatives—always the thin hands holding the precious thing
firmly, but in such a way as not to obscure any part of it.
In one only a single finger—I thought the left little finger,
but with a negative it takes a bit of working out—had come
right across the folded edge of the foot. It was the clearest
negative of the lot, but had not been used. The finger wore
a ring.

I squinted through the tiny transparency, trying to see
what the ring would look like in the positive. There was a
square dark centre showing white in the negative, possibly
a square-cut ruby or sapphire, with some indeterminate
detail round it. The hoop itself seemed triple, at any rate
near the bezel. That was the best I could do.

I started to put the envelope back in the drawer, changed
my mind and put it in my inside pocket. I could not think
what further use the negatives could be to me, once I had
seen them, but I did not see why the secret, such as it was,
that I now shared with old Levinson should go any further.

I shut the drawer and leant gingerly across the desk. I
turned back the pages of the desk diary to the 12th of June.
It carried, in Levinson's unexpectedly untidy hand, the one
word 'Dunstreet'.

I turned the pages back, leant across to the telephone and
dialled 999.

19

3

Levinson died of natural causes and left his entire collection to the Victoria and Albert. Apparently neither was unexpected. The doctors knew his heart was weak, and the trustees had a copy of the codicil. The collection was fully and expertly catalogued, and did not contain the Verzelini tazza. He left his books to Peter Sarrett, who must have had most of them already. There was the usual large family no one had ever heard of to take care of the money. Everything was quite in order, only now nobody knew where the tazza was. His papers contained no reference to it, and no trace was found of the photographs, except for the prints sent to *Old Glass* with his report.

This took a weight off my mind. The negatives and the envelope had all gone into my stove, except for the tiny fragment containing the ring finger, which I enlarged until it started to lose all definition. It still did not tell me much. A square-cut, dark-coloured stone surrounded by some sort of chased work, presumably gold, and a thin hoop that spread out into a triple fan on each side of the bezel. That, the name Dunstreet and the date was all I had. But nobody else had anything at all. And nobody knew I had even this. I took my colour-twist to Cecil Davis, who said it was Dutch.

I sat in my room in the evenings till long after it was dark, thinking round and round the thing. I had to assume that, at least by the time Levinson photographed it, the owner knew what she had got. I say 'she', because the owner of the tazza was presumably the owner of the hands, and the hands certainly looked feminine. Apart from their size and

20

shape, only a woman could wear a ring like that. It was not, perhaps, completely safe to assume that she knew all about it, but Levinson must have offered some explanation for wanting to photograph it. The fact remained that she had not parted with it and was still lying low. Besides, I did not think Levinson would have left things unexplained. Levinson was not like that.

This left several possible lines of enquiry. There was the Levinson line—Levinson's own connections with Dunstreet, his movements on and around 12th June, and so on. There was what you might call the glass line—any sort of interest or dealings in old glass near Dunstreet, local collections or sales. And there was the ring—the strongest possible pointer, but with only one chance in a million of its turning up. Last, and much more problematic, there was the possibility of a historical connection, hitherto untraced but traceable, that might account for the thing's existence and present whereabouts.

The glass world went into a brief ferment over the tazza. Even the ordinary press took an interest, and one of the popular dailies ran a story under the headline 'Queen's Treasure Disappears', but killed it next day. No one could be absolutely certain the thing existed, still less what it would be worth if it turned up; and in a world jaded with enormous prices only an outsize quotable figure could make news for long. For the expert, Peter Sarrett settled the thing very neatly in an obituary note in *The Times*.

No one, he said, knowing the extent of Levinson's expert knowledge and his personal integrity could doubt that the tazza existed. It was incumbent on us to respect the reasons, no doubt weighty, which had led him not to disclose its present whereabouts and ownership. It must be assumed that the thing was somewhere in private hands and that the owner wished it to remain there. Now that its existence and authenticity had been established, it would no doubt in due

21

course be brought forward when its owner wished it to be so. There could at least be no longer any danger of its being neglected or destroyed for want of appreciation of its true significance and value. For this, and for our knowledge of its existence, we were indebted to Levinson. For the rest, we must await its owner's pleasure.

This was putting a bold front on it, and was indeed the only line Peter could take. 'But what do you really think?' I asked him. He had slapped me down over the thing once, and I was not going to have it happen a second time. I looked at him with a sort of confidential cynicism which I knew he would dislike intensely. 'Why did the old boy publish the thing like that if he knew he couldn't tell the whole story? Of course, he couldn't know he was going to die within a week of publication. He may have been keeping something up his sleeve for purposes of his own.'

I knew this would annoy Peter, and it did. He had no sense of humour in anything that concerned *Old Glass*. His eyes protruded slightly, and his whole dark face was full of outrage. He said, 'I suppose it doesn't occur to you that it may have been precisely because he expected to die soon that he published as he did?'

I raised my eyebrows, but said nothing. I was sitting in his flat drinking his gin, and I felt there must be a limit even to deliberate provocation.

He frowned. 'You wouldn't understand his attitude,' he said. 'I knew Levinson pretty well. He was—a scholar, if you like. Once he was satisfied the thing existed, he had to establish the fact as far as he could. Obviously he was under some constraint from the owner not to publish names and places. A lesser man might have taken one of two other courses. He might have waited in the hope that the owner would allow him to publish full details; or he might have ignored the owner's wishes and gone ahead and published them. I think it was typical of him that he did neither. He

22

felt bound to establish the facts as far as he was allowed to do so. The fact that he might die at any time made it more imperative, not less. He couldn't let the knowledge die with him.'

I said, 'So it was, in fact, the owner who prevented him from giving details?'

His face did not change at all. He said very quietly, 'I have already told you—I don't know that. Levinson told me nothing more than was in his report. But it seems the most likely assumption, especially knowing Levinson.'

'So the thing must be left as it is until the owner relents?'

'Obviously. What else?'

'You could make some enquiries, couldn't you?'

'How? It's not just a matter of trying to get in touch with the owner. The owner already knows the facts and isn't going to come forward—we must assume that. We shouldn't know where to start.'

This seemed to me very satisfactory, and I left it at that. I did at least know where to start. At Dunstreet. What to do when I got there I did not yet know. But that would come.

The garage was round at the side of the house. There was a very pale saturnine man polishing a very dark, upright car with a sort of respectful energy. The car was perfectly in character. It was a car for old-fashioned nobility or elderly royalty. I did not see what could happen now to prevent its being bought by an undertaker. It was a cortège in itself. But it must still be lovely to drive, so long as you could afford the petrol.

He had a black band on his dark blue sleeve, and I spoke with a proper sympathy. Levinson would have been a wonderful employer. I told him who I was and explained my predicament. I had been upset—he could understand that—and to tell the truth a bit rattled. I must have left the

23

books in Mr Levinson's room, and they were library books I had to return. Did he think—?

He said perhaps I had better ring up and speak to Miss Joachim. She was not in now. Tomorrow morning would be best. I said I would.

'That's a beautiful car,' I said. 'Don't see many of these on the road now. How long have you been driving her?'

He nodded solemnly. 'Since we had her,' he said.

'Mostly in town, I suppose. Or did Mr Levinson travel much?'

He thought about this while he polished. 'Not what you'd call travel,' he said. 'He used to get about a fair bit.'

'Did he ever drive himself?'

'Not often. He could, though. He was a good driver, Mr Levinson. But he was beginning to find the traffic a bit fast for him. He didn't like to go fast himself, not even with me driving.'

It was my turn to nod, and I nodded. 'I wondered,' I said. 'I knew he went down Dunstreet way last month. Some friends of mine met him. I wondered if he drove himself.'

He stopped polishing and looked at me. He said, 'When was this, then?'

I said, 'About the middle of the month. Fifteenth, perhaps. No, a bit earlier.'

He nodded again, but this time to himself. He said, 'Dunstreet, was it? To tell you the truth, I wondered where he'd been. Took the car himself. The twelfth, it was, he went and came back next day. He'd done all of three hundred miles in her by the time he came back, and I wondered, naturally. He didn't often drive that far himself.'

'No,' I said. 'Pretty good for a man of his age. Well, I mustn't keep you. I'll ring up tomorrow, as you suggest. Unless I find I've left them somewhere else. I may do, yet.'

We nodded mutually and simultaneously, and I walked

24

round the corner and wrote down the number of the dark upright car. I never had a head for this kind of detail, especially when it is important. But I knew one thing. A man who looked like Levinson driving a car that looked like Levinson's car would have been pretty conspicuous anywhere. If he had gone where I thought, he must have blazed a trail as definitive as a railway track. I went home and got out my maps. As I had imagined, Dunstreet was just short of a hundred and fifty miles from London. Then I got the A.A. book and looked up the hotels. There was, virtually, only one. Dunstreet was not tourist country, not really; the great caravan route to the west ran twenty miles or more to the north of it. It was near enough the sea, but not the sort of sea people went to. The *Fleur-de-Lys* got three stars. The *Swan* got one and the rest were nowhere. It was as simple as that.

For my money, the *Fleur-de-Lys* was worth all its three stars. I got there at the awkward hour of five o'clock, and the man in the hall said, 'Hullo, sir,' as cheerfully as if he had lent me a fiver five years ago and not seen me since. The girl at the desk had huge green eyes and a voice like dripping honey. I got a room at the back, facing out over a huddle of slate roofs to a long dark ridge hung to its whole height with oaks. They looked so thickly grown that you could walk on the tops of them.

I dumped my case and took the car out again to explore. The whole countryside was dark green and crouched a bit. There was pasture and some corn on the higher ground, but the trees filled all the valley bottoms as if they had been poured into them—as indeed, in embryo, they probably had—and the valleys ran together in a network always pointing southwards to the place where their combined streams met salt water almost between the oak roots. The air was so soft and wet you could squeeze it out. It smelt of

25

dead wood and land-locked brine. I found it all extraordinarily exhilarating, but it obviously lacked tourist
attractions. The houses were dark stone and slate, each
buried in its cluster of trees. At intervals, in the breaks of
the hills, I could see rubbed down stone towers that looked
like derelict mine workings. I was not surprised the tazza
had turned up here, if this was where it had. I should not
have been surprised to find a derelict merchantman rotting
somewhere under the hanging oaks complete with a contra-
band cargo of Venice glasses.

As I turned back into the town the word 'Antiques' drew
my eye with the smooth compulsion of a hurrying blonde.
This time it was a notice of sale. Messrs Truscott and Scarworthy announced their summer auction of Furniture,
Antiques and Objets d'Art, including, in smaller type, a
Jacobean Oak Dresser, a Marquetry Card Table, Georgian
Box Toilet Mirrors, a Square Waiter of 1729, four Salts
with Crest 1763, Dresden, Derby and Staffordshire Groups
and Figures and an Interesting Early English Ale Glass
with Engraved Bowl, etc., etc. The date was next day and
the time 10 a.m.

I could think of nothing nicer. From what I knew of these
local auctions, the dealers of the next three counties would
be there for a bloodless carve-up, ready to buy anything
at a price that would allow them a thirty-three per cent
mark-up and still find a buyer in the holiday season, or
when the bigger sharks came down from the tourist centres.
The private buyer, if he intervened, would be taken scientifi-
cally to the current retail price and dropped there in the
interests of trade. The thing could be full of pleasurable
excitement if you knew what the current retail prices were
and what a local dealer looked like. I thought I knew both.

Also, sporting interest apart, anyone in Dunstreet who
was interested in glass interested me, and the auction was
an opportunity I should be both foolish and churlish to

miss. I put the car away and found the Queen Street Auction Rooms where the sale was to be. It was long after viewing hours, but I flattened my nose on the narrow windows picking out, among the dusky masses of *objets d'art*, the Square Waiter, a Box Toilet Mirror and two more than usually repulsive Staffordshire figures, but not the Interesting Ale Glass. I reckoned a quick look round at half past nine and a little intelligent use of the catalogue ought to put me in fighting trim. I did not, by the sound of it, want anything there, not even particularly the Ale Glass, and this would leave my pleasure unadulterated by the pangs of competitive desire.

There was no need for devious enquiries about Levinson. I simply found the hotel garage man and mentioned the upright car, and he remembered it at once. 'Gentleman with a beard,' he said, 'old chap and dressed very old-fashioned. Only stayed one night. Very pleasant spoken, though.' I took this to mean that Levinson, as one would expect of him, had tipped well. I could not hope to get into the Levinson class, but I spoke as pleasantly as I could, and he seemed satisfied.

The *Fleur-de-Lys* might have got a fourth star if they had hired a London head waiter and frenchified their menu. As it was, the head waiter had an elderly man's version of the desk girl's honey-drip, and the cook had probably been brought up in the kitchens of the local gentry. I ate a clear soup called clear soup, ribs of beef, apple tart and cream and Stilton. I will not pretend that I drank beer instead of Burgundy, but apart from this—and Burgundy is an international institution, not a local mystery—I would not have changed the food for anything available from Moscow to San Francisco. I suppose my tastes are insular.

I went to bed early and looked out in the last of the daylight at the massed oaks on the far ridge. Somewhere, not far off in this salt-smelling, tree-tunnelled countryside, a thing I sweated to think of had kept its brittle fragility intact for more than four hundred years. Someone—one person, I imagined—knew it for what it was and had got Levinson down specially to look at it. Everything pointed to that—the sudden, unaccompanied journey, the caginess, the suppression of the documentary evidence, even a single letter, that must have existed. And now Levinson was dead, and whoever it was would think no one else knew anything. And here I was, full of London wickedness and the local food, lodged in perfect comfort next to the heart of the mystery.

I sighed luxuriously. The sour, soft air came cold in my nostrils, and I was wonderfully happy. I slept perfectly and was brought strong tea in a blue and white teapot at seven in the morning.

4

I picked up a catalogue from the table by the door and
dropped two sixpences into a strictly non-Georgian salver.
I walked between the polished surfaces, over the Kirman
and Tabriz rugs that littered the floor, to where, at the far
end of the room, the silver and glass was housed in glass-
fronted shelves which themselves carried lot numbers in the
corners. The whole thing was unexpectedly impressive. I
am no judge of furniture, but this was obviously the real
stuff, emerging under the pressure of steadily rising prices
from the homes that had housed it for generations. It was
stained and patched in places, but still essentially as it had
left the craftsman's shop, with the superadded patina of
time. The silver was the same. I was touched, as always, by
the pathetic and tantalising scarcity of the glass.

There is no patching or soldering of glass, no hammering
it out into shape and repolishing it. One moment it is there,
tensile, vibrant, full of its own mysterious stresses and
voices, and the next it is irrecoverably ruined, dead for ever.
Every moment of an old glass is a moment borrowed from
long overdue destruction. The miracle of its creation is
almost superseded by the miracle of its survival.

There were four glasses of the great period here, against
hundreds of ounces of silver and a large roomful of woodwork. I could not see, I never could see, how anyone in his
senses could buy anything else while the glasses were still
for sale. Not that any of these was anything special. There
was a noble facet-cut wine with what the trade irreverently
calls the Oxo pattern cut round the lip of the bowl. There
was a pair of rather dingy white twists which I did not

examine, but thought were foreigners. And there was the Interesting Ale. It was not, in fact, particularly interesting, but wonderfully beautiful. A tall, slender thing, with a single-knopped air-twist stem and a design of hops and barley exquisitely wheel-engraved on the bowl. I had one very like it and had seen several others. If I could have had it for a reasonable price I should have bought it just so as not to leave it in the wrong hands. But reasonable prices were out. There was no mistaking the atmosphere or the faces.

There was a facet-cut woman with an iron grey shingle that was itself, in its way, a legitimate period piece. There was a rubbery man with rather long curly hair and little darting eyes. More formidable still, there was a dark-faced, balding man in a plain dark suit, who stood motionless, propped against a gilt wall mirror, looking at nothing. Unless I was very much mistaken, he had come to buy one piece of furniture, and would buy it, not regardless, but fairly reasonably, because the others, who all knew who he was and where he came from, would know it was no use bidding against him. There were at least two hearty couples muttering cheerfully to each other in voices that sounded like the Critics. These were not amateurs, but new dealers, still getting fun out of it and ready to pick up what the bigger predators did not particularly want.

The mere public was, of course, represented. People looking for wedding presents, brides furnishing, businessmen who had bought ancient houses with architect-designed central heating and wanted particular pieces to go in particular places. Innocents who had fallen in love with one lot. They were formidable because they were ignorant and enthusiastic. The subtle fury of the auction would get a grip on them, and they would wave their catalogues compulsively at figures away beyond the prices they would have to pay at a respectable dealer's. Above all, they did not need to re-sell at a profit to make a living. They were cushioned by a relentless rise in prices, and did not have to kid themselves to know that, whatever they paid, the thing would be worth more in a few years' time. The dealers would see to it that they paid the current retail price: but the dealers could not, by the logic of their trade, outbid them if they were determined to buy.

I expected the auctioneer to be old, but he was not. He came of a new generation of Truscotts or Scarworthys, or had married into them. He was small and ruddy. He had a small moustache over a rather sad little mouth and brown ox-eyes that surveyed the company with a sort of melancholy surprise. But he knew his business.

He made a small, competent speech in the local language. He said he was pleased to see so many old friends there. He looked with mild expectancy at the hatchet faces of the dealers bowed over their carefully marked catalogues. Only the curly-haired man showed any sign of having heard him. He also welcomed several newcomers, and his brown ox-eyes sized me up, wondering what I was interested in and what I was good for. He said they had some really nice stuff there and expected nice prices for it, so he hoped we wouldn't waste his time with five shilling bids. The big room was packed now, what with the lots and the bidders, and the feeling of expectancy pressed in on the small central space, where the girls sat at their ledgers under the rostrum. It was cosy compared with Christie's or Sotheby's, but it was surprising, in the middle of that lost landscape, how much they had in common.

'Well,' said the auctioneer. He flexed his arm elaborately and looked at what, in that setting, would be a gent's handsome gold wristlet watch, seven jewels. 'Ten o'clock,' he said. 'A few minutes after. Let's take Lot No. 1.'

The early lots are never very exciting. The real bidders may arrive late and those who are there have not yet

31

warmed to the job. The amateurs are still embarrassed by the unexpected tension and the sound of their own voices. Things go cheap, and nothing of importance is allowed into the first half-hour or so.

A matronly woman, probably the bride's mother, bought an oak table for three pounds ten. It was too large to put in a corner and too small to eat at, but might have its uses. She seemed overcome by her bloodless victory and gave her name in an uneasy whisper. A mahogany wardrobe came up, pointed out by an assistant in a far corner of the room and obviously too heavy to be shifted elsewhere except by a full team of experts. The auctioneer looked at it speculatively. 'Nice roomy wardrobe, that,' he said, and asked for a bid of two pounds. After several seconds of silence a roomy man bid thirty shillings and was promptly raised to two pounds by an obstinate-looking man opposite him. Hotel-keepers, I thought, with a new annexe to furnish. Possibly farmers, but I did not think so. They drove each other, ten shillings at a time, to four pounds, and an unseen woman from the back came in at four ten. Quite suddenly, battle was joined. The faint, unconscious murmur of an audience taken out of itself greeted each bid, and the neutrals looked expectantly from one contestant to the other. Only the dealers were unmoved. They waited with pencils poised over the middle pages of the catalogue. The men, rivals in other respects, shared a determination not to let the woman outbid them, and one of them raised her immediately every time she spoke, till the roomy man found himself left in at six pounds. The tension collapsed as suddenly as it had risen, and the auctioneer, too experienced to be surprised at anything and too professional to show any surprise he may have felt, knocked the wardrobe down in dead silence and went on to the next lot.

After the first half-hour the real antiques started coming up, and the dealers, using only a flipped catalogue or a

32

lifted eyebrow, were suddenly in there, making most of the running. The bride's mother, still breathless, was taken carefully to twenty-five pounds for a small chest she had obviously hoped to get for about fifteen ten. One of the businessmen joined issue with the curly-haired man over the marquetry card-table. At thirty pounds his director's voice suddenly became pure Lancashire. He bid forty-five and was disconcerted at the sudden silence. The curly-haired man, smiling very slightly, was turning over the page as if he did not know marquetry existed. Ox-eyes brought the hammer down quick, and Lancashire fumbled aggressively for its cheque book. The dark man still had not moved or spoken.

The glass came up just before lunch. I had mentally left the white twists to their fate, but was determined to see justice done to the facet-cut and the ale. I had put a retail price of seven ten on the wine and fifteen on the ale. The bidding, I saw from the start, was purely professional, and when the wine paused at five, I raised it to five ten. Curly-hair and the grey shingle both raised their eyes from their catalogues simultaneously and gave me a quick but comprehensive look. I smiled with friendly simplicity at the auctioneer. Curly-hair gave the faintest sigh and suggested six. I hesitated, smiled nervously, swallowed twice and said six ten. Ox-eyes came in, looking at me with mild interest, and asked if there were any further bids. At the last moment the grey woman said seven. I caught the eye of a dark girl standing on the far side of the room and could swear there was mischief in it. She did not say a word. Nor, at this stage, did I. The grey woman was left in at seven, and I wished her joy of any profits she could get on it.

The auctioneer announced the ale. 'Very interesting glass, that,' he said. 'Beautiful. Look at the engraving.' Curly-hair opened at three. I raised him to four, and one of the couples, smiling excitedly at each other, said five. I looked

33

at the dark girl. I wanted to make sure. Without raising her eyes from her catalogue she said, 'Ten.' Her voice was splendidly vibrant, but her face was quite expressionless. 'Ten, thank you,' said the auctioneer. 'That's better, now.' The soft brown eyes turned for a moment to the dealers on his left and Curly-hair flipped his catalogue. 'Eleven,' said the auctioneer. I let it lie for a bit and then said, 'Twelve.' The dark girl raised her eyes and for a crowded second looked full into mine from under her arched dark brows. Curly-hair came back with thirteen and there was a long pause. The auctioneer said, 'Well, then. Thirteen I'm bid. Is there—?'

The dark girl said, 'Thirteen ten.'

I looked at her. 'Fourteen,' I said. She was very self-possessed and desperately attractive.

Curly-hair, finding two of us still in, said 'Fourteen ten,' but his voice was slightly apprehensive. The dark girl gave me another long look, and this time we both smiled. With the mutual assurance of a pair of bridge-sharks we left it. Curly-hair bought the interesting ale at fourteen ten and consoled himself by buying the pair of enamel twists for seven. He could do well on those with an unwary buyer. The auctioneer announced an hour off for lunch.

I steered myself across the stream of drifting bodies and we came alongside as we reached the door. She must have been in her late twenties and was nearly as tall as I was. The street was full of damp sunlight, but her skin was flawless and almost unpowdered. We smiled sideways at each other. She said, 'I didn't want it, either.'

I said, 'Lunch?'

'That would be very nice.' She was absolutely sure of herself. She said, 'I don't know—do you know Dunstreet?'

I shook my head. 'Just visiting,' I said.

'There's only the *Fleur-de-Lys* really, unless you go further out.'

'I'm staying there,' I said. 'I find it good.'

'Are you? Yes, I think it is.' We walked off down Queen Street, mentally arm in arm.

The man in the hall had abandoned his baize apron for a semi-full-dress uniform jacket, but was still very friendly. He said, 'Good morning, Miss James. Good morning, sir. Sale going well?'

I said, 'Very well, thank you,' and we moved in to lunch.

'I don't need to ask the obvious question,' I said. 'You clearly live here. And your name is James.' She wore no ring of any sort. I could not imagine how a girl like this had reached her present age without someone getting hold of her.

She nodded. 'And you, on the same evidence, are down for the sale. Only you haven't bid for anything yet, except to make the dealers pay for those glasses.'

'No,' I said, 'it breaks down there. The chap in the hall—'

'Henry,' she said.

'All right, Henry. Henry no doubt knows we were both at the sale. Nothing very difficult in that. But in point of fact I only found out about it when I got here yesterday evening.'

'But you managed to take time off for it?'

I said, 'Oh yes,' but did not say time off from what.

The *Fleur-de-Lys* lunch was well up to expectations. A joint, a bird, a pie and a pudding. The pie I know was superb. The bird looked good and Miss James said it was. To complete my happiness they produced a beautiful Gewurtztraminer.

Miss James tried again. She looked at her watch and said, 'Time's getting on. They start again pretty sharp at two.'

I said, 'Are you going?'

She looked at me with her head a little on one side. It was pretty shameless but completely charming. 'I don't know,' she said.

'I'm not.'

'No longer interested?'

'Not in the furniture or silver. Still less in the *objets d'art.* I admit I should like to know what the dark man's after.'

'By the mirror?'

'Yes.'

'He's London. It may be some of the silver. Or I'm told there's one bit of Dresden that's very good.'

'He's welcome to it.'

'If it's glass you're interested in, why didn't you buy the ale instead of playing poor old Fosbery for it?'

'Curly-hair's Fosbery?'

She nodded. 'Charles Fosbery, Antiques. Swincombe, back on the A.30. I must say, I thought it was lovely.'

'I've got one very like it. I'd have bought it cheap, gladly. But nothing's going to be cheap with that lot of sharks in.'

She put her head on one side again. She said, 'You collect, but not professionally?'

'More or less. And you?'

'I don't collect, no. I'm very interested. Do you know a lot about it? I should think it could get a bit of a hold.'

'It does. It's an addiction. I haven't actually murdered anyone for a bit of glass yet, but it's only a matter of time.' I told her about my Newcastle and the Midland junk shop.

She looked at me, straight this time. She said, 'You didn't actually hit him?' It was so like David I laughed outright.

'I'm sorry,' I said. 'You reacted so exactly like a friend of mine. He said the same. He then warned me solemnly against further violence, but I must say he was very nice about it. He collects himself, of course. We do a lot of mutual coveting.'

'This is in London?'

I nodded. 'He's a civil servant, and a little bit earnest. But he's got some lovely stuff.'

36

'Do you know all the London people?'

'My fellow addicts? I know most of them.'

I wondered about Levinson, but hesitated. Her eyes were in her coffee cup. It was long past two. She looked up suddenly and said, 'I must be going.'

'Not back to Queen Street?'

'Not there, no. But I have my life to lead.'

We made our way out. She said, 'I've enjoyed it very much.'

I stood square in front of her. 'I should like to see you again,' I said.

She stood there looking at me, her eyes almost level with mine. She might have been thinking. My belief was that she had already thought. You could never catch this girl thinking, but she thought all the time, even with her head on one side.

'Yes, all right,' she said. 'Are you going to be here long?'

'I don't know. Not very long.'

'Come and have a drink tomorrow evening. Lower West Street. Twenty-three. A green door. Ignore the doctor's surgery. I'm on the first floor. Say about six.'

'Thank you very much. I look forward to it.'

At eleven next morning I drank a horrible cup of coffee in Swincombe High Street and turned into Charles Fosbery, Antiques. Mrs Fosbery's hair was not curly at all, or if it was it was not given much play. I did not think she had been at the sale, and certainly hoped not. There was in fact no recognition. I said, 'Have you anything in the way of drinking glasses? Anything eighteenth century. A twist for choice.' There was no room for subtlety here.

Mrs Fosbery looked at me, wondering what I was good for. She said, 'There's a red and white twist there. I don't know—'

I looked at it and smiled at her. I said, 'Not that one, I

think.' It was dreadfully wrong. This told her what she wanted to know, and she produced yesterday's pair of white twists. 'We've just had these in,' she said. 'They're a pair, but I expect they could be separated.' They were marked six guineas each. I looked at them carefully. They were eighteenth century, all right, but foreigners, as I had thought.

I said, 'Anything in the way of an air-twist?'

She was all set now. 'There's one very beautiful one,' she said. 'That's just come in, too. An ale. I'll get it if you're interested. I'm afraid it's very expensive.'

'I'd like to see it anyhow.'

She went and got it. Charles Fosbery was evidently still licking his wounds and had not put a price on it yet. I wondered what she'd say. It was a beautiful thing. And yesterday it had been mine, certainly, for fifteen. It was going to cost me a bit my not knowing, round about one o'clock, what I had known by half past two.

I said, 'Yes, that's nice,' in my most appraising voice. 'What are you asking for it?'

Mrs Fosbery was no Midland junk merchant. She spoke without compunction or doubt. 'Twenty guineas,' she said.

I raised my eyebrows, but went on examining the glass. Finally I said, 'It's nice, yes, but I think twenty is too high.'

She said, 'I could make it pounds.'

'I'll give you nineteen for it. That's really a very good price, you know.' It was. Mrs Fosbery knew it, and by this time she was fairly certain that I knew it. But she would have liked to ask Charles.

'Oh dear,' she said. 'All right. Nineteen, then.'

'Pounds,' I said.

She sighed. 'Pounds, yes.'

She wrapped and boxed it and I set out for Dunstreet and the *Fleur-de-Lys*. I did not sing this time. I did not want to. I knew Miss James would like it, but I did not know at

38

all whether she would accept it or whether, if she accepted it, she would tell me more about her interest in glass and in due course more about her interest in mine. There were a dozen things, on several very different planes of thought, I wondered about Miss James. The Interesting Ale might help. But I still wished I had bought it yesterday.

5

At six o'clock I presented myself to Miss James at 23 Lower West Street with my parcel in my hand. Just before eight darling Claudia re-positioned herself a little breathlessly but decisively and said, 'It's time you went, Johnnie.'

I am not at all sure, even now, by what stages this transformation came about. The trouble certainly started when, having neither strong ale nor an eighteenth-century taste for it, we filled the tall glass with mainly brandy and began using it as a loving cup. A long neglected glass is always glad to be drunk out of, and the Interesting Ale may have done its best for me. By eight, or a little before, the glass stood safely in the middle of the mantelpiece—nothing could make me neglect a precaution like that—and I was fairly inextricably entwined with Claudia. It was at this point, as I have said, that she told me to go.

I said, 'I can't go now. The party's only just starting.'

'That's a different party,' said Claudia. 'I didn't know you'd been invited. This one's definitely over.'

I fell back on the defeated man's classic line. I said, 'Claudia darling, you can't do this to me.'

Claudia said, 'Well, you can't do that to me.'

'But think what sort of a state you're leaving me in. Both of us, damn it.'

'I have thought. Hungry.'

The pale cast of thought that had sicklied over my native resolution took on a rosier colour. She was, in fact, perfectly right. I was already beginning to doubt whether she was ever wrong. I was starving.

'All right,' I said. 'This party's over. The other is adjourned, but not *sine die*.'

40

Claudia sat up and said, 'That will be the *dies*.' She went to the nominative without hesitation. She was not called Claudia for nothing. I think I fell in love with her from that moment. All I said was, 'Where do we eat, then? The *Fleur-de-Lys* again, or is there something more exotic?'

She was by the mantelpiece, straightening herself in a huge gilt mirror. She said, 'I don't know what you mean by exotic. Do you like lobster?'

'Do they do lobsters round here?'

'I think they discovered them. The Romans would never have gone on with their invasion if they hadn't got here and found the British eating them. It's all wrong about the oysters.'

'And you would never have been called Claudia. It makes you think. Yes, of course I like lobster. Not too much messed about. Just cooked.'

She nodded and went to the telephone on the corner table. She dialled straight through to a local number and said, 'Mrs Pargeter?'

The phone clucked and she went on, 'Mrs Pargeter, it's Claudia speaking. Have you got a lobster?'

Mrs Pargeter sounded indignant, even across the room. Claudia said, 'That's wonderful. In about half-an-hour. What? Yes, two of us. Goodbye till then.'

She said to me, 'I think you'd better get your car and bring it here. You drive and I'll navigate. I'll be ready when you get back.'

Henry said, 'You dining in, Mr Slade?' I felt I had lived there all my life. I said, 'No, I'm going out.' He was full of vicarious anticipation, but all he said was, 'Right, sir. I'll tell them.'

Claudia appeared from the door in Lower West Street exactly as I pulled up. She climbed in beside me and said, 'Straight on through the town and follow the main road till I tell you.'

41

The light was already going. After a quarter of a mile or so she said, 'Next left. It goes down steeply.' The lane was marked Cartery. It was high-banked, and the trees closed it in completely overhead. I switched on the side lights.

We drove steadily, forcing a cylinder of damp air through the tunnel ahead of us and sucking in other air, equally dead, behind. Nothing else moved, but I saw a gleam of water through the crowded tree-stems on my left. Presently the trees parted altogether, and we came on a long arm of flat water, leaden and motionless between the hanging trees. Everything smelt of salt, but it was as much like sea-water as a municipal swimming bath getting on for closing time.

Then we turned uphill again, and a moment later there were stone cottages on both sides and even a few figures moving. A red sign, curiously bright and freshly painted in that grey street, said 'The Ship', and Claudia said, 'Here. You can pull in beyond the door.'

We went from the dusk of the street into the darkness of a flagged passage and then out through a door into a totally strange daylight beyond. There was a stone terrace with a sea wall and a slip going down under it. Beyond, and as far as I could see ahead, there was a whole world of level grey water under a luminous grey sky. On both sides the land leant on the water in lifeless masses of trees. The air was soft, and there was a table set for two against the sea wall.

Mrs Pargeter popped her head out of a back window and said, 'There you are, dear. Ready in ten minutes. All right?'

She ran an appraising eye over me and popped back. I could not resist the impression that I was a guest artist at a regular performance, but it did not worry me. There was a sort of suppressed exhilaration in that dank air and the curious left-over daylight.

We leant on the sea wall looking down at a couple of boats which rode motionless on running moorings. 'I'm in your hands,' I said. 'What do you propose we drink?'

'It will have to be beer. There is no fine food nonsense about the Ship. But it's a nice clear bitter, and you'll find it goes as well with the lobster as anything you could think of. If you want a short one first, there's gin. Not for me. It's food I want.'

I looked at that sharp, perfect profile silhouetted against the shadowy woods. It had a dreaming quality that her unwavering concentration on lobster and clear bitter could not dispel. It went with the silence and this timeless world of dark trees and fading water. I have travelled as much as most people, but I have never felt more out of the world than I did during those few minutes before Mrs Pargeter brought the tray.

The tray held two plates, each with half a good-sized lobster on it, a bowl containing lettuce, chives and parsley, all mint-fresh, a brown loaf, a slab of butter and a squat glass jug of pale-golden beer. The accessories were already on the table, including one of those oil and vinegar twins with the bottles leaning drunkenly across each other.

During the next hour or so the magic, if anything, increased in intensity but changed its quality. When the light went, Mrs Pargeter brought a couple of candles. They were set, not quaintly in ancient brass or roguishly in empty bottles, but in the enamelled bedroom candlesticks I remembered from a very, very long way back. The flames did not flicker except when we laughed or the moths came too close to them.

I knew all about lobster, but I still had something to learn about beer. We drank a second jug of it and leant again on the sea wall, leaving the candles burning on the table behind us. Mrs Pargeter came out and in the proper eighteenth-century manner offered us tea, which we refused. Coffee was not mentioned. She looked slant-eyed at Claudia and said would we like a drop of something.

Claudia said, 'Oh yes, please,' and she brought two verit-
able tavern drams with trumpet bowls and firing feet filled
with something that ought to have been very expensive
but probably, at Cartery, was still not. We sipped it leaning
on the wall, with the candles burning steadily behind us,
and talked about everything except each other. I took the
glasses and put them back on the table to be safe. When I
came back to the wall, our arms touched and we kept them
so, just in contact, and I should not have minded whether
the sea under the wall was the Arctic Ocean or the South
Pacific so long as our arms were touching.

Finally she said, 'Shall I pay?'

'I wish you would. I'm out of my depth. Will this cover
it?' I gave her some notes and presently she came back and
gave me the change. I never knew what the meal cost,
except more of my peace of mind than at my age I could
safely spare.

We said good night to Mrs Pargeter and went to the car.
'Don't turn her,' said Claudia. 'We'll go out to the point
and back by the main road.' I pulled her to me and kissed
her before we got into the car. I have never felt such peace
or so strong an assurance of it. Then we followed the head-
lamps into the tunnel of trees again, until there was a
natural movement of air in our faces, and we heard a live
sea, which we never saw, breaking monotonously on an
endless shingle beach on our left hand. The road ran
straight in a gentle switchback for several miles, and all the
time, like True Thomas and the Queen of Elfhame, we saw
neither sun nor moon, but heard the roaring of the sea.

Then the road turned inland again, going in long curves
over high ground that smelt like moorland. I saw only two
spots of light on the road at first, rising and falling steadily,
and then two more, moving at a quicker rhythm, but
smaller or farther back. The buck came straight down the
middle of the road at full stretch and never swerved a foot

44

either way. He was mad with whatever was behind him and quite blind from the lights in front. Only at the last moment he lowered his head and came full tilt into the front of a car already skidding under my violent braking. There was a crash and thud and we stopped dead, with the lights, mercifully, still blazing down the road ahead. There was complete silence, but after a moment I could hear a breeze from the sea rustling very gently the heather or whatever it was that stretched away on either side of the road.

We both got out and looked at the crumpled brown heap half under the car. There was some blood on the road. I got back quickly into the driving seat. The car had to be backed off anyway, and I had to get away from that broken body. Something clung to the car for a bit as I backed and then slumped off. I did not go back more than a foot or two, so as not to bring it into the headlights.

Claudia stood in the light of the nearside lamp, looking down. Then she stooped, caught hold of something and pulled at it. Her expression was quite impassive, with a touch of irritation in it. She let it go and came round to the nearside door. 'Come and give me a hand,' she said.

I sat where I was. 'I can't,' I said. 'I'm sorry. Can you manage?'

She put her head in at the open door and smiled at me. She said, 'How now, my lord, a soldier and afeard?' She was very cheerful.

I shook my head. 'I'm no soldier,' I said. 'It's just a thing I have.'

She took her head out without saying anything and went back to the front of the car. She stooped again, and then I saw, standing in the full glare of the lamps, the owner of the second pair of eyes.

I do not know what sort of hell-hound it was that conducted its own private stag hunt in the dark over that wild country. It was just a big dog, very square in front. I could

45

see the hackles all down his back, and he grinned at Claudia, with a gentle continuous bubble of growl in the back of his throat. I began to shout to her, but at the same moment she straightened up and saw him.

She grinned back at him and walked a step or two in his direction. He put his head down, holding his ground. Then she spun round, stooped and picked up something off the ground. She swung it up, and I saw it was a complete antler, snapped off short near the socket. There was blood on the broken end.

She went for the dog with it, lunging and sweeping at him savagely, and I could hear her cursing him in a quiet, carefully enunciated stream of wicked words. He drew back under the sudden fury of the attack and then gathered himself and jumped round her, feinting and snapping at her. The two of them kept up a steady stream of soft, furious sound. Then she changed feet quickly, like a fencer, and went forward in a long thrust. The branching tines caught him in the face, and he let out a squeal and turned tail. He went off down the road howling in a long diminuendo that had more rage than pain in it.

Claudia stood there, her feet spread wide apart, for a moment, and then let out a clear cackle of triumphant laughter. She walked back to the car, swishing her horrible trophy and smiling through the glare of the lights into my face, which she could not see but knew was watching her. She whirled the broken antler and flung it away into the heather. Then she stooped again and took hold of the invisible deer. She put out a sudden strength and dragged it clear, so that they disappeared together from the light of the lamps, and I heard rustling and threshing noises in the rough stuff at the roadside.

I turned off the headlights and sat there, with only the glow of side lights in front of me. My knee shook as I put the clutch down and disentangled the gears from the stalled engine. I restarted the engine, and a moment later Claudia opened the near door and got in beside me. She was breathing quickly from her exertions and smiled gently to herself.

She said, 'Poor Johnnie. Never mind.' I put the car in gear and moved off. There seemed to be no mechanical damage. She turned to me and drew a finger softly down the left side of my neck, under the ear. It was a caress, with unmistakable affection in it, but when she took her finger away the skin felt cold where she had touched it.

I drove faster and faster over the long switchback, seeing nothing but the road stretching away into the tunnel of light in front. There was no light anywhere else. I could not get True Thomas out of my head. It would have been just this sort of breathless, lost darkness, and they had ridden through blood above the knee. It is, in fact, less than five miles from the point beyond Cartery back to the main road just outside Dunstreet, and the road runs straight all the way. It seemed a very long drive.

The houses began all at once, and then the street lighting. I was surprised to find the pubs still open and people about in the streets. I stopped the car outside the door in Lower West Street and turned to Claudia. We had neither of us said a word since she had touched me, and I do not know quite what I expected to find. I found a very smooth, self-possessed young woman, who turned to me smiling when I turned to her.

She said, 'That was a wild ride. The devil wasn't really after you, you know, Johnnie.'

'He was,' I said. 'I left him.'

She pulled my head down to hers. 'I'll deal with him,' she said.

'I don't doubt that,' I said it obliquely, but the peace I had felt before flowed out of her and changed my meaning while I spoke.

'When are you going back to London?'

I had not been conscious of any intention, but I said, 'Tomorrow, I think.'

'No luck?'

'Not so far.'

'You can come and see me, though, can't you, sometimes?'

'Oh yes, I'll come and see you.' I was not expressing any intention, merely stating a fact.

She moved away suddenly, opened the door and got out. She said, 'Thank you for the meal. It was lovely.'

I said, 'Thank you. It was out of this world.' That was a fact, too.

The car was badly dented and had dark stains. There was no one about in the hotel garage, and I got water and a cleaning brush, and attacked it fiercely. I left it clean but still battered.

Henry, who was never off duty, saw my hands and said, 'Had trouble, Mr Slade?'

'Hit a deer,' I said. 'Killed him, I'm afraid. And bashed up the car a bit.'

He clucked. 'It happens quite often at night,' he said. 'The lights dazzle them. Did you bring him back?'

I shook my head and he clucked again. 'A pity,' he said. 'They can be very good eating. And when a thing's dead, it's dead.'

'I suppose so.' I had no intention of explaining my predicament to Henry. I went upstairs and shut myself into my room. I could not think of anything except Claudia, and her not at all clearly. I went to the mirror over the basin, and worked feverishly with soap and water long after I had in fact got rid of the rust-coloured smear down the left side of my neck.

I had not given the tazza a thought since six.

48

6

Mrs Larkin said, 'That Mr Sarrett called.' She had known Peter Sarrett as long as I had, which must have been going on for ten years now, but she never missed an opportunity of calling him that Mr Sarrett, as though she were looking at him through the wrong end of a sort of moral telescope. I never knew why she disliked him so. I was not particularly fond of Peter myself, but I could never see how he offended against any probable principles of Mrs Larkin's. He was a bachelor, and the fact that he devoted every third thought to *Old Glass* would not, I suppose, make him in her eyes gainfully employed. But the same could be said of me and my writing. She probably, in fact, disapproved of me, too, to a certain extent, but I gave her very little trouble, and she had overcome her scruples for the sake of good labour relations.

'He come in,' she said, 'walked straight in while I was doing my cleaning and asked where you'd got to. I told him you hadn't consulted me before you went, and even if I did know I wouldn't tell him nothing.'

I knew perfectly well she had said nothing of the sort. What Mrs Larkin was recounting was a sort of dream incident in which her heavily idealised relations with me had clashed sonorously with the general unreliability she longed to rebuke in Peter Sarrett. All she had in fact done was to look down her nose and tell him she did not know when I should be back.

I said, 'Oh well, he always walks in if the door's on the latch. He knows I don't mind. When was this, then, Mrs Larkin?'

49

'Yesterday, in the morning.'

'I'll give him a ring and reassure him.'

She left that, visibly, between me and my conscience. Then she brightened up. 'And Mr Bruce rang this morning,' she said, 'from the office. His secretary come on first, and asked who I was and I told her. Then I heard her tell Mr Bruce and he said, "Oh yes, I'd like to speak to Mrs Larkin".'

Mrs Larkin's version of David's̄ manner of speech, though it hardly did him justice, was evidently meant to flatter. She liked David as much as she disliked Peter, and the incident, with its implicit status symbols, had evidently made a very favourable impression.

'Yes?' I said. 'And what did he say when he did speak to you?'

'He said to tell you if you come back today any time to come round and have a drink with him and Mrs Bruce and stay for a meal if you could. I said I'd tell you if you came back, or leave a message in case.'

'Thank you. That's fine.'

'Will you be going then?'

I do not generally stand up to Mrs Larkin, but this was so gross a violation of my privacy that I said, 'I don't know. Why?'

She looked as if a piece of cake had suddenly bitten her back. 'Why?' she said. 'Well—it would be nice for you, wouldn't it? That nice Mrs Bruce.'

David's Daphne was that nice Mrs Bruce as regularly as Peter was that Mr Sarrett. She fulfilled so exactly Mrs Larkin's idea of the wife I ought to marry that if I had told her I was going to live in sin with Daphne until David divorced her, I am sure she would have said, 'What, with that nice Mrs Bruce?' Not that this seemed in the least likely to happen. Daphne Bruce embodied all the arguments in favour of marriage when one was feeling in a

50

marriageable mood, and all the arguments against it when one was not. She was educated and attractive and capable and companionable and absolutely impossible to get away from. I was very fond of her as David's wife, and she gave me the sort of affectionate, tolerant, semi-deprecatory treatment that a married woman like her naturally accords a man like me. I took full advantage of this when I was so inclined, and in the intervals thanked my stars for the situation of honourable celibacy.

I saw Mrs Larkin off, still ignorant of whether I was going to spend the evening with that nice Mrs Bruce. Mrs Larkin put in a reasonable part of five days of the week with me, but was not the companion of my nights. She presumably fulfilled this role for Mr Larkin, who I knew existed but who was otherwise a rather shadowy figure. She was as discreet in respect of her own private life as she was avid for indiscretion in respect of mine. When she had gone, I sat down for a peaceful concentrated think about Claudia.

The results were, in fact, unsatisfactory. Considered in retrospect from arid, over-lit London, Claudia and the haunted countryside of Dunstreet and Cartery assumed so persistently the characteristics of a dream that it was very difficult to think about them logically. Reasonable speculation slipped into fantasy at the drop of a hat, and fantasy seemed just as likely to be true.

As it happened, no logical decision was needed. I should in any case be going to Dunstreet again soon, because that was where my line to the tazza lay. And if I went to Dunstreet, I should in any case see Claudia, if for no other reason, because I could not keep away from her. The only thing I might have given constructive thought to was how to deal with Claudia when I saw her: and I already knew enough to know that any plans I made were likely to go by the board in the face of either a totally unexpected Claudia

51

or a totally unexpected reaction on my part to the Claudia I had planned for.

I mixed myself a drink to dull the edge of my restlessness. When I had drunk it, I rang up Peter. He was in.

He said, 'Oh, hullo, Johnnie. I called to see you yesterday, but you weren't at home. Your woman told me she didn't know when you'd be back.'

'I hope she wasn't rude to you?'

'Rude? No, why should she be?'

'Why, indeed? Only by her account of the matter I was afraid perhaps she might have been.'

'Not rude, no. A bit unforthcoming, perhaps. Didn't know where you were or when you'd be back—that sort of thing.'

'I know. As a matter of fact, she didn't. She wasn't holding out on you, I mean.'

'No, of course not. Why should she? I didn't imagine you'd told her your movements under a seal of secrecy.'

There was a pause. At this point I should have said, 'As a matter of fact, I'd only run down to Worthing to see an aunt,' or something of the sort. In fact I said nothing, and all the time I was saying nothing Peter waited at the other end to see what I was going to say.

Finally he said, 'Well, anyway—why not come in and have a drink this evening?'

If I hesitated, I believe it was only the sheer temptation of being able to tell Mrs Larkin that I had rejected the invitation of that nice Mrs Bruce in favour of an evening with that Mr Sarrett. But the temptation was not strong enough. I did not want to spend the evening with Peter. I said, 'I can't, I'm afraid. I'm dining with David and Daphne. But I'll be seeing you some time, certainly.'

'Yes. All right. You're staying in town for a bit?'

'Oh yes, so far as I know. I've got no fixed plans, anyway.'

'I see. All right. I'll be seeing you, Johnnie.'

I put down the receiver. It occurred to me some time later that I did not know why Peter had come to see me and that he had not explained.

Daphne had put on a very elegant short black frock that threw up in surprising detail her rather full but very desirable contours. Her golden hair was sleek, the children were silent upstairs and there was a faint and pleasant smell of food from the kitchen. To say that this was all for my benefit is inevitably to sound conceited, but there is, in fact, no conceit in the matter. Daphne always did her best with me, not only in the domestic way, but even as a matter of straight sex. Like many women who are triumphantly married, she liked nothing better than to show unmarried men what they were missing. I used to wonder what would happen if I were suddenly to take all this coming-on at its face value and (presumably in David's absence) lay lascivious hands on her, which God knows I was at any time inclined to do. I thought she would be thrilled for about five seconds and thereafter horrified and probably virtuously indignant. As I knew this, and she knew that I knew it, she felt free to play her hand for all it was worth. David took no notice of it, beyond a curious mixture of cynical amusement and slightly smug complacency.

Daphne said, 'Hullo, Johnnie,' in the curious flat intonation affected by the young things at the time when she had been a young thing.

I said, 'Hullo, Daphne.' I smiled warmly into her wide green eyes and did not touch her. We were neither of us of the generation that kissed cheeks and called each other darling. We knew too much for that.

'Where have you been off to?' said David. 'It's not fair. You have too much time on your hands and you're too mobile. No wonder you find things.'

53

'It's no good finding things if one hasn't got the money to buy them,' I said. 'You can't have it both ways. You may not get around as much as I do, but look what they pay you to stay still.'

David said, 'How much of my pay do you think I'm allowed to spend on glass? Anyway, did you find anything?'

'No,' I said. 'I saw a nice air-twist ale, but they wanted twenty quid for it, and I've already got one very much like it.'

'Where did you go, anyway?'

I said, 'I went down to Worthing to see an aunt.' David looked at me. He laughed and said nothing. Daphne was at my elbow with my whisky. She handed it to me over my shoulder, so that I smelt her forearm. 'You are a wonderfully dutiful nephew,' she said. 'And wonderfully ubiquitous. One or both of your grandfathers must have been a terrific man in bed.'

'Both,' I said. 'My maternal aunts in fact slightly outnumber my paternal, but they lack their warm family affections and geographical distribution.'

Daphne said, 'The Worthing aunt is clearly paternal. Such is her family affection that she has left a longish hair under your left lapel. Judging by its glossy blackness, she must be a very young aunt, or very well preserved.'

'Both,' I said again. 'My father was the eldest of a very long family—you know all about my grandfather's activities —and some of my younger paternal aunts might well be my cousins. And the Worthing air is wonderfully preservative.'

I felt Daphne's fingers on the stuff of my jacket and grabbed at them. I did not want that nice Mrs Bruce, sleek and golden and town-bred, to have Claudia's hair in her hand. Daphne snatched it playfully, and my hand shut on her fingers with a strength neither of us had expected. She said, 'Oh—Johnnie!' and David's head came up with a snap. He said, 'What—?' but Daphne said, 'It's all right.'

She stood over me, undeniably magnificent in her cling-ing black, and looked at me with a curious mixture of indignation and excitement. All the time she was uncon-sciously massaging the fingers of her right hand with those of her left. She said, 'Sorry, Johnnie. I didn't mean to provoke.'

I grinned at her. 'That's all right, Daphne,' I said. 'I didn't mean to be rough.' The hair must have stayed where it was, because later when I got home I found it and put it between the handkerchiefs in my top drawer. I was in that sort of state. At the time all Daphne said was, 'You're a mysterious character, Johnnie. You and your aunts.' David said nothing.

We dined on something very simple and tasty in a cas-serole and a very pleasant dry table wine. David contributed a fascinating account of a bureaucratic involvement at his Ministry. He made a very good thing of it, but earnestness kept breaking through. I gave them a worked-up version of the Dunstreet auction, which I placed a couple of months back in time and somewhere in the Welsh marches. It was a nice evening altogether.

The test came, as always, when I got back to the flat. It was always one thing or the other after dining with the Bruces, which I did most weeks. Either I dived in through the door as gratefully as an animal into its burrow and found everything very friendly, the books waiting to be read, the light and heat waiting to be turned on, the chair waiting to be sat in. Or I stepped into an unfamiliar and even hostile place that some other man, never myself, had quitted and left his things in, like my things but irretrievably different. It is purely subjective, of course. I have hired a hotel room for a single night and come back to it at the end of the evening as if it were the home of my childhood. Some

55

evenings do that to you. Others leave you simply unfit to be left alone. When it was the Bruces, it was a question whether dear, damned Daphne had got under my defences with her little ways. As I have said, she never stopped trying and I never for a moment let on how often she succeeded.

On this particular occasion the thing was curiously double-edged. I would have settled for Daphne, or anything else in well-filled black, to round out my fireside, but I did not want, as I sometimes quite consciously did, something simple in a casserole and children asleep upstairs. I wanted lobster and the dank smell of lost sea-water. My restlessness had been held at bay but had not left me. The flat I had come back to was not properly my own.

My suitcase, still half unpacked, was on the bed. I did not encourage Mrs Larkin's ambitions to be a *valet de chambre*. Not being much of a man for clothes, I had taken my only decent dark suit straight out of the case and put it on to go to the Bruces'. Hence, of course, the hair under the lapel. The rest of the stuff was much as I had packed it at the *Fleur-de-Lys*.

I began to take the things out and put them away. I had to, if I wanted to get to bed, and I am obsessively tidy over my personal possessions. My sense of unfamiliarity increased as I did this. I was putting the things away in the other man's flat. His things were like my things, but he did not keep them exactly as I had kept mine. I tutted a little over his occasional untidiness.

I got it all away at last and stowed the suitcase where it lived in the spare room cupboard. I gave myself a whisky and soda for a nightcap and started to get to bed. I was in my bath when I began wondering about the whisky decanter. Surely not Mrs Larkin? I had always assumed that she was above the classic temptations, and there had never been anything to shake this assumption. It was not the whisky, now. I had no idea how much there had been in the decanter. It was the decanter itself. I kept it and the others in a corner cupboard, rather crowded with bottles and glasses and the other apparatus of proper drinking. The decanters were in the front rank, the most needed where they came most easily to hand, and the whisky immediately in the opening of the door. It occurred to me, looking back, that it had changed places with the gin, which I hardly ever touch when I am alone. Looking back, I mean, with the mind's eye, because I was in the bath and was not going to pad across the flat in a damp towel to settle a doubt about Mrs Larkin.

The restlessness was dying out of me and I was getting sleepy. I almost dozed in the hot water, and my mind came up with an association between Mrs Larkin, the whisky decanter and a grey sweater in the crowded bottom drawer of my chest-of-drawers. I pulled myself together and got myself out of the bath, dry and into the towelling dressing-gown I kept hanging on the bathroom door. Awake and on my feet, I did not really suspect Mrs Larkin of trying on my sweaters, though the result might have had a certain fascination.

I went to the corner cupboard and found the gin under my hand and the whisky further along the rank. A sense of disquiet settled in my stomach. I could not bear the thought of having to watch the levels in my decanters and the other things that went with it. For the moment both these particular decanters were nearly full.

I did not open my bottom drawer. I knew that the old grey sweater, which had sunk to the bottom from long disuse, was visible at the top of the drawer, but this no longer seemed important. I went into the bedroom, my right hand jangling the keys of the flat in my dressing-gown pocket.

7

It was blowing great guns in Lower West Street, which made
it very different from the last time. There were leaves
everywhere, not dead leaves yet, but tired leaves with not
much resistance in them, which the wind had ripped from
the threshing hangers and carried into the town. It was
getting on for noon, and Claudia's door was locked and
unresponsive. Whatever it was she did all day, she was
away doing it.

The *Fleur-de-Lys* had a coal fire burning in the saloon
bar and there was a rumble of local voices over pre-lunch
noggins. I put my head in cautiously and met the melancholy brown eyes of the auctioneer. It was only a sort of
swivel shot in the direction of the open door. His eyes went
straight back to the solid black-coated man he was talking
to. He said, 'No, but I mean, you've got to be reasonable.
It's no good asking us to sell a place and then putting a
reserve on it no one's going to bid. They all expect to make
their fortunes, that's the trouble. Well, some of them do
very well. But as I say, every house isn't a gold mine, even
these days.'

I said to Henry, 'That chap in there—the one who did
the auction the other day—would he be a Mr Truscott or
a Mr Scarworthy? Youngish chap, small moustache.'

'That's Mr Pridham.'

'No Truscotts or Scarworthys?'

'There's Mr Charles Scarworthy. Old gentleman, he is.
Don't see him in here very much.'

'No Truscotts, anyway?'

Henry looked doubtful, as if he had put some Truscotts

down somewhere but could not put his hand on them. 'Don't think so, Mr Slade. Or not that I know of. Mr Scarworthy runs the office and Mr Pridham does most of the selling.'

'He comes from round here, though, doesn't he?'

'Not from round here, no. Tranton man, he is.'

I nodded. Tranton could not be more than twenty-five miles from Dunstreet. It was a matter of scale, really.

I went into the saloon with a proper diffidence, nodded deferentially to the company and pulled up at the end of the bar away from the fire, with my face towards Mr Pridham. The ox-eyes came round to me, hesitated and went away again. I still had not really seen the black-coated man, but he had bank manager written all over his shoulders.

Mr Pridham returned to his previous theme. His voice, like his face, was full of gentle melancholy at the unreasonableness of other people. 'As I say,' he said, 'you've got to be reasonable, no matter whether you're buying or selling. If you haven't got the seller's price and the seller won't shift, you can't buy.' His sad smile came over the black shoulders and included me. 'This gentleman will tell you,' he said. 'Unless I'm mistaken, he was bidding the other day, but I don't think he bought anything.'

The bank manager half turned. I smiled and took my glass over. 'You're quite right,' I said. 'Your prices were a bit high for me. On what I wanted, anyway.'

Mr Pridham nodded. 'I thought so,' he said. 'Glass, wasn't it?'

'You've got a remarkable memory,' I said. 'You're perfectly right, of course.'

He gave a deprecatory smile. 'Well,' he said, 'we know most of the regulars, you know. When one sees a fresh face, one remembers it. Matter of fact, I took you for a private collector, but you got out so neatly I wondered.'

I shrugged. 'I've got a few bits I won't part with,' I said. 'Most of us have that. But I deal all right. Only at the proper price, of course.'

He nodded, looking at me with mild speculation. 'But you're still hoping to find whatever it is you want in these parts?'

There was only one answer to this. 'Oh yes,' I said, 'I'm still hoping.' I had a feeling, as I said this, that someone had asked me the same question once before, but I could not place it. I said, 'There must be plenty of old stuff around. How does it reach you?'

He thought, looking into his glass. I suddenly remembered Claudia saying, 'No luck?' I had said, without thinking, 'Not so far.' Now I wondered what she had meant.

'It happens several ways,' said Mr Pridham. 'People die, of course.' He looked at me to see if I would challenge this. I nodded and he went on. 'Then sometimes people have a thing for years and never give it a thought till they see something like it sold for a nice bit. Then they think, "I wonder what that old piece is worth?" They don't mean to sell, not at that stage. But once they've started wondering what a thing's worth, it's on the way out. After a bit they take it to a dealer and ask him. He'll make them an offer, if the thing's any good. They aren't going to accept—not then. But it puts ideas in their heads. They think, "You can't trust these dealers".' Mr Pridham smiled at me apologetically. ' "If he offered a couple of quid, it must be worth at least a fiver." That's what they think. And of course often they're right. Then they'll lay off until something turns up and they need the money. Then as often as not they bring it to us to put in one of our sales. By that time they can't wait, and if there's no sale coming off soon, back they'll go to the dealer again, or to a different dealer, and ask for a couple of quid more. But if there's a sale, they think they'll get more for it that way.'

He smiled at us again, apologising for the processes of human greed which he detailed so relentlessly in his soft voice. 'Or there are the ones who know a thing is worth a fair bit, but hold on to it till they're pretty well desperate for a bit of cash. Old people, mostly. They're the worst of all—for us, I mean. Nearly always think the thing's worth more than it is. The fact is, they're only selling because they think so. And of course if they can't get the price they have in mind, they get furious. But they sell in the end. It's always the same. Well you know yourself. Once you've put a monetary value on a thing in your own mind, you aren't going to keep it long. You don't want it any more, you see? Not really. It's the money you want more. Otherwise you'd never think of it.'

I said, 'But the stuff is there?'

'Glass, do you mean? Not much, now. It gets broken. But there's always liable to be the odd bit in the old houses. No good looking in the new ones, or the ones that have been spruced up. Any old stuff there is there for what it is, and they don't want to part with it. In the old houses it's still there by chance, where it's always been, and they may be ready to sell. But there's no getting anything cheap. There's more people now think a thing is worth twice what it is than don't think it's worth anything.'

I said, 'Some of these houses round here you'd think hadn't changed hands for centuries.'

Mr Pridham shook his head. 'You'd be surprised,' he said. 'Of course, there are the old families.' He smiled at the bank manager. 'Old Miss Barton,' he said. 'I bet you'd find some stuff out there if you knew what to look for.'

For the first time the bank manager spoke. His voice was just right. Not local originally, I judged, but localised from long residence and much talking to farmers. 'I dare say,' he said. 'Not that I've ever been there. But I believe there've been Bartons there for three hundred years at least, and I suppose there must be a lot of old stuff around. I shouldn't know it if I saw it, I'm afraid.'

'Not that Miss Barton needs to sell off the heirlooms, I imagine.' Mr Pridham looked speculatively at the bank manager and the bank manager looked at nothing.

'That the oldest local family?' I said.

'Oh yes,' said Mr Pridham. 'Always been Bartons here. But the old lady's the last of them. And I don't suppose she'll last much longer.' He got down from his stool. 'Well,' he said, 'let me know if you find anything. I'd be interested to hear.' I do not know where the others lunched, but it was not at the *Fleur-de-Lys*.

I turned into the end of Lower West Street just before six and saw a dark green Morris 1000 pulling away from the door. I did not know who was in it, but I accelerated and went after it. If it was not Claudia, I could always come back. There is only one set of traffic lights in Dunstreet and it turned red between the Morris and me. I watched the Morris go off in the direction we had taken that evening, but whether it was making for the Cartery turning I could not tell.

The lights changed and I went after it again. There was no sign of it at the Cartery turning. I reckoned the Morris must have gone too fast to be going to Cartery, and I held on along the main road. I drove fast by my standards, but it was not road-racing stuff. From what I knew of them, the Morris could go every bit as fast as I could, and it certainly had not been wasting time.

The road came out over a crest and plunged into a tree-filled valley. On the far side, where it climbed clear of the trees again, I saw something just disappearing over the top. It might or might not have been the Morris. At least there was something on the road ahead of me. I charged down into the wind-torn tree-tops, dived under them and roared up the other side.

62

It was the Morris all right. I saw it clearly for a couple of seconds before it turned sharp left and disappeared into the trees again. There was a finger post which said 'Grane'. I did not know what Grane was but that was where I was going. Judging by the size and quality of the road, it was nothing special.

The Morris must have been going slower now, as well it might, because when the road stopped weaving between the tree trunks and straightened out for a few hundred yards I suddenly saw it not far ahead. My hand went to the hooter, but I did not press it. Instead I slowed down and let the Morris disappear round the next bend. I had no very coherent intention, but I no longer wanted to catch it. I still did not know whether Claudia was in it, but, in case she was, I wanted to see where she was going.

There was still tarmac on the road, but it was not much more than a single track with rough edges. I drove more quietly now, and was conscious for the first time of the threshing of the dense-packed, spindly trees on either side of me. We had been going downhill gradually for some time, but there was still no water.

There was a turning off to the right, but I did not see it until I was almost past it. It was even narrower than the road I was on, and went off into the trees on a sharp left-hand curve. I saw the back of the Morris on the curve, and as I saw it, it moved off again out of sight. I braked, skidding to a halt on the loose metal that cluttered the edges of the narrow tarmac. I backed, turned into the side track, took the curve as fast as I could and came, incredibly, to a further fork. Both sides looked alike. Neither was signposted. I stopped right in the crutch of the fork. There was nothing anywhere but grey trees, grown too close together and lashing at each other furiously with their dull green leaves. There was nothing even to suggest which way to go.

I still did not know who was in the Morris. I backed my

car rather violently round the fork and drove back to what
was, in a very limited sense, the main road. I did at least
know where that was going. Grane. But I could not see
much purpose in going there myself. I turned left and went
back the way I had come. I drove slowly, and wondered.

At the first reasonably wide stretch a dark green Morris
1000 drove straight past me in a smooth rush. There was
no mistaking the profile. This time I hooted and kept my
hand down. The Morris pulled in to the side. I pulled in
behind it, got out and walked to the offside door. Claudia
was peering up at me with an expression of polite enquiry.
Then her face changed completely. If I live to be a hundred
and grow older in my folly all the time, I shall still think
she was pleased to see me.

She said, 'Hullo! What are you doing here?'

I said, 'Where are you off to?' simultaneously.

We both waited for the other one to reply. I waited longer
than she did. 'Dunstreet,' she said.

That was undeniably true. 'Where from, then?' I said.

She smiled up at me ravishingly from the driving seat. If
the door had been open, I should have kissed her mouth
while it was still smiling. 'Dunstreet,' she said.

'Just driving round?'

'That's it.' The woods moaned and threshed round us.
The sky was clear over the narrow road. This time a week
or so ago it had been almost dusk, but now it was only a
rather cold daylight. She repeated her question. 'What are
you doing here?'

'Just driving round. This your car?'

She nodded, still smiling. I said, 'I tried to find you this
morning. Lunch-time, anyhow. But you were out.'

'That's right. I had gone to see my aunt.'

I said, 'Not you too?' but she was perfectly serious, and
my question puzzled her.

She said, 'Me too what?'

'Aunts,' I said.

'Not aunts. An aunt. I more or less look after her.'

'I hope she is a rich aunt.'

'Oh, I think so, quite.' She looked beyond me at the tormented trees. 'Don't you think this is a bit cheerless?'

I said, 'Greenland's coast.'

'Yes, I know. But we've got two cars here. Surely one or both of them could get us to Dunstreet.'

I sighed. 'It will have to be both. You drive on, I'll follow.'

'You're sure you won't get left behind?'

'Nothing short of a heart attack or mechanical breakdown. You just try.' She nodded, and I walked back to my car. She switched on her side lights and drove on sedately along the narrow winding track between the now darkening woods. I followed the pair of twisting rubies in a state of pleasant semi-hypnosis. It seemed no time at all before we came to the turning off the main road, where the finger post pointed back over my shoulder to Grane.

Just before we got to the Cartery turning I had an idea. I hooted sharply three times. She slowed down and I slid past her and in to the side of the road. I walked back and said, 'What about lobster?'

'Not tonight. I can't. I'll give you a quick drink and then you must go back to the *Fleur-de-Lys*.'

I still leant on the side of the car. 'Tomorrow?' I said.

'I think so. For the moment let's go on, don't you think?'

I went back to my car, and the moment my door was shut she was past me and off towards Dunstreet. For the second time I lost her at the lights, and when I pulled up in Lower West Street the green Morris was not there. I walked up and tried the door. It was shut, but a moment later I heard her clacking up the stairs behind me.

The Interesting Ale still stood splendidly in the middle of the mantelpiece, but tonight we let it stand. She gave me a drink in an ordinary glass, and I put it down and took hold of her. I had forgotten what she smelt like. She said, 'What brings you to Dunstreet?'

'You,' I said. I said it into her hair.

She backed off and looked up at me. 'Me and what else?'

'The devil that drives me. The devil drives me and the enchantress draws me, and between the two I can't keep away.'

She said, 'You must go now, anyway. Swallow that drink and be off.'

'Tomorrow?'

'All right. Six. Here.' I swallowed my drink and went.

8

I finished my first cup of strong sweet tea and stared at the ceiling. The wind had gone, I noticed, but it had left an unusual freshness in the air that felt like autumn, even in bed.

If Claudia had been going to Grane, I thought, it was time I went there. This did not mean that yesterday's decision to turn left and not right had been wrong. At that point I had not known for certain that the dark green Morris was hers. Also, I had a feeling that whichever way I had gone after turning back at the fork in the woods, before very long the Morris would have shot past me, and Claudia, by merely sitting in it and smiling up at me, would have driven everything else out of my head.

The fact remained that Claudia had taken the Grane turning, and I could not believe that that road went any-where else. As for the turning off to the right, the left prong of the fork at least must lead back into the Grane road again, or she could not have been on my tail so quickly after I had abandoned the chase.

I drank a second cup of tea. I wondered why it was that a brew I would never stomach at home was acceptable, and even pleasantly stimulating, in a back bedroom of the *Fleur-de-Lys* at half past seven in the morning. I came to the conclusion that it was because I had not made it myself. I wondered if Daphne made David a pot of tea in the morning, and tried to imagine her bringing it in in a quilted dressing-gown. Not that she needed quilting. And in any case he probably made it for her. Claudia's dressing-gown would be something dark, with a matt surface and zipped up to the neck. I was going to see Claudia that evening at six. Perhaps even, in due course, her dressing-gown. There is room for hope in all things, and most hope has an element of apprehension in it. I got up and started to dress.

I took the Grane turning soon after half past ten and drove with a vacant mind until I came to the turning off right, which I missed again, as I had the day before. It was, on closer inspection, not much more than a gap in the trees. I might as well settle one point at least. I backed, turned into it and took the left fork. It was hardly more than a lightly metalled bridle-path, and, as I thought, it set back in a long left-hand curve towards the direction of the Grane road. I was some way along it when I remembered, or thought I remembered, hearing a car on the road behind me after I had turned off it. But then even the Grane road must be used by somebody. If anyone lived at Grane, whatever it was when you got there, they might well need bread and butcher's meat at least. Unless they slaughtered their own beasts and dressed in the skins, which did not seem impossible. A moment later my track edged coyly out on to a slightly wider road which ought, I supposed, to be the Grane road, but had no distinguishing features of any sort. On yesterday's timing the distance was about right. If Claudia had come along here full bat and then turned back left-handed, I reckoned she would have caught me just about where she had. I could, of course, turn back left-handed myself now, and see.

I turned right, or rather followed the line of my track out on to the road, and drove on. Now the road dipped much more sharply, and I suddenly caught the expected whiff of salt. It was slighter and fresher, as if yesterday's wind had cleared out an accumulation of stagnant air, but there was no mistaking it. I still could not see water.

Some time later there was a turning off left, going sharply downhill. I missed it, hesitated, stopped the car and walked back. I went down it on foot and saw why I could smell the water but not see it. I was almost on top of it. Just here the land, instead of sliding gently down into the intruding sea, plunged into it almost vertically from about thirty feet up. It was quite a wide creek, and at the moment full of water. I could not see how deep it was. All I could see was reflected sky between the trees. A moment later I was in fact over it. There was a bridge. It seemed to be all wood and might have put down roots. On the seaward side of it, or so I judged, the creek ran out fairly straight and parallel with the road above it. On the other it curved away right-handed into the dark earth and hanging tree-roots, still looking quite deep. There was nothing to say where anything went. I walked back up to the road and got into the car. I was still going to Grane, and that meant following the road, such as it was. Whatever Grane was, it could not lie across that wooden bridge.

I still do not know what Grane properly consists of. The road climbed suddenly clear of the trees and ran out on to a long low promontory with blue sea to the horizon. There was a sea-mark of some sort on the highest point, and near the point a cove had a small jetty half across it and a couple of stone cottages with no sign of life in them. It was very like what I imagined the point beyond Cartery was like in daylight, but that must be several miles eastward. My road turned the point and showed every sign of making back to the main road away inland. I turned the car and drove back.

I left it where I had left it the first time and walked down to the bridge. There were car tracks on both sides of it, but nothing to show whether it was a public road or private property. The bridge was sound enough. The tide had risen slightly since I had first seen it, and there looked to be ten or twelve foot of water in the creek. I crossed the bridge and began to climb the other side. The road ran up in a tunnel of overgrown trees. It was like the other roads I had driven over in these parts, but I had not walked on one before, and a car is a great insulator. It was dead quiet, and I did not like it. There was nothing under the trees but moss and occasionally fleshy plants with coloured berries. Everything smelt of rotten wood.

The road turned right in a hairpin bend, and the next moment the trees fell back a bit and there was a solid bank of rhododendrons on each side. There might have been flowers on the tops of the bushes, but all I could see was dark green waxy leaves, that moved only when I touched them. The road looked more like a drive now. It ran straight ahead for sixty or seventy yards. There was nothing to see except the rhododendrons, but the whole place had an intolerable air of privacy. I think if I had heard anything coming from the far end of the road, I should have turned tail and run for it, or even dived under the bushes and hidden until whatever it was had gone past. But nothing stirred, and I kept on walking.

I saw the chimneys through a gap in the bushes on my left. They had red pots on tall stone stacks, and were so decisively below me that if I had been closer to them I could have flipped a pebble down into them. In fact they were twenty yards or so away. I pushed between the bushes and looked down. The road ran on top of a green bank, fringed with rhododendrons at the top but clear of trees below. The house stood at the bottom of the bank, with its back turned to it. Almost all I could see was a huge expanse of grey-slated roof. On my right the drive plunged sharply round the far end of the house and came round in a carriage-sweep in front. Everything else was trees. There was no smoke in any of the chimneys and no smell of it in the air. Somewhere, very faintly, I heard somebody talking.

It was a woman's voice, very high-pitched and monotonous. It was quite impossible to hear what she was saying, but she was somewhere down by the house. She could have been in front of it, with her voice, even down under the far wall of the house, shut in in that great well of silent trees. Wherever she was, I could not see her, nor she me. I stepped back between the bushes and went on down the drive, walking as quietly as I could. I followed the drive round the end of the house and then, forcing a way cautiously between the bushes on my left hand, looked along the front.

The carriage-sweep was of grey gravel, clear of weeds and marked by the circling tracks of car tyres. The house was all of the dark local stone. It was neither beautiful nor ugly, neither dilapidated nor spruce. It was static, neutral and non-committal. I cannot pretend, even looking back, that it horrified me, but it was dreadfully oppressive. The front door must have been open, though I was too much on one side to see. That was where the voice was coming from, and presently the owner of the voice walked out on to the gravel. She was still talking.

She was a tall, soldierly woman with a frame much too big for that little thin, continuous voice. She wore a bunchy black skirt with a long apron over it and some sort of blue and white blouse on her great square top half. I think if her voice had been of a normal pitch I could have heard what she was saying from where I was. Everything else was completely silent. As it was, I could hear an almost continuous stream of sound, articulated and inflected like speech, but defying my analysis. She walked out into the middle of that grey gravel sweep, stopped and looked all round at the sky and the silent trees. Then she turned and went back into the house again. The door shut with an unnecessarily violent bang and the voice was cut off.

I tried to remember what her face was like, but could form no picture of it. Almost against my inclination, I dodged back into the bushes and followed the drive round to the front of the house, where it ended in the circular

71

sweep. Half behind the last rhododendron bush I peered with a sort of unwilling curiosity at the windows, one after the other.

They had lace curtains in them, old-fashioned but neatly draped and as far as I could see clean. Nothing much was visible behind them. I worked along all the windows on both floors, starting at my end, but saw nothing. When my eyes came back to my end again, there was a woman standing between the curtains in a first-floor window looking straight at me. I thought at first it was the woman I had already seen. She looked every bit as tall, but there was no apron, and the whole dress was black. Both had grey hair rather elaborately arranged. I still could not remember the first face at all, but the face I was looking at now was surprisingly vivid, even at this range. The brows were black and arched over unusually round eyes. I could not see the colour, but they looked pale. Even full-face, the nose looked aquiline and imperious, but the mouth under it was curved in a long, close-lipped smile that took it right round the sides of her head. There was nothing particularly repellent or formidable in it, but it was an unnerving face.

For a second neither of us moved. Then I dodged back behind the bush and began to walk up the steep curve of the drive. At the point of the curve, level with the end of the house, I stopped and listened. There was still not a sound anywhere. I walked quietly up to the straight stretch, looked back, saw nothing and fairly took to my heels. I do not think I was afraid in any coherent sense. I just wanted to get away as fast as I could.

I was not in any particular condition for running, and by the time I flung myself down the dark tunnel of trees and out over the bridge, I was desperately short of breath. Once across the bridge I was all right. The water behind me was broad and even among the tree roots smelt of the sea. My sense of escape was no more reasonable than my urge to escape had been, but it was nice to have it.

I got into the car, started it up quickly and set out for Dunstreet. I had been driving for some minutes when I knew that I had heard a car start up behind me and that it was still there.

I slowed down almost to a crawl, but nothing appeared behind me. I turned a bend, accelerated through the gears as quick as I could make the car move and shot off along one of the comparatively straight stretches. Just as I came to the end of it, I thought I saw a car in my driving mirror, coming into the straight at the far end. It looked like a Morris, but I could not get any colour. I drove on until I came to the left-hand turning that led to the fork. I made sure the road was clear behind me and then backed and flung the car round into the narrow track. I drove to the fork, backed, turned and drove back almost to the Grane road again. Then I waited.

Nothing happened and no one came. I waited a good ten minutes, feeling increasingly angry and increasingly foolish. Then I pulled out on to the road and made straight for Dunstreet.

I was outside Claudia's door at six, and heard a piano playing inside. It was Chopin with so much *rubato* that one wondered why whoever it was bothered about the Chopin. Claudia was wearing something dark, matt and zipped up to the neck, but it was not a dressing-gown. She went to the wireless in the corner, hesitated and switched it off. She said, 'I don't think that's very good, do you?'

'No, I don't. Who is it?'

'A woman called Jennifer Marsh. She's had a tremendous write-up. I can't think why.'

'If you'd seen her, you'd know. Very attractive piece, wonderful figure, sways about at the piano like a sea-anemone in a flood-tide with long shiny hair swaying in the

73

opposite direction. She hit the country a few months ago and got around the critics as fast as her legs could carry them. No wonder she's been acclaimed. All except old Cassell, who's more interested in male sopranos.'

She came back from the wireless and stood in front of me. She said, 'You're rather horrible, Johnnie. I like you, but I can't help feeling there's something rather horrible about you. I wish I didn't.'

'Look,' I said, 'you can't blame me for what the Jennifer Marshes and the critics do. Better be horrible to her than let her be horrible to poor old Chopin. Where were you this morning?'

She had been turning away towards the drinks, but she stopped and turned back to me. 'Swincombe. Why?'

'What were you doing in Swincombe?'

She did not waste time being indignant and asking what business it was of mine. She looked me very straight in the eye and said, 'Shopping.'

'For your aunt?'

'Yes. Would you like to see my receipts? My aunt likes to have them.'

'Yes, please.' She went to a drawer and took out a neat cash account backed by a small sheaf of vouchers. They were all Swincombe shops and of that day's date. I said, 'Could have been this afternoon.'

She shook her head. 'Early closing. The A.A. book will tell you.'

I handed her back the papers and sat down. I said, 'It's no good saying I'm sorry.'

'None at all. But I confess to a certain curiosity why you behave as badly as you do.'

'I think someone spent the morning following me.'

'And you thought it was me?'

'I thought it was your car. And it was where I met you yesterday.'

74

'On the Grane road? You were out on the Grane road this morning?' I nodded. 'Where did you go?'

'I don't know. To the end of the point and back. I don't know if I got to Grane or not. Claudia—' I took her hands. She let me take them, but they were completely passive in mine and rather cold. 'You really have got an aunt, have you?'

'Oh yes, I've got an aunt all right.'

I said, 'There you have the advantage of me.'

'I should have thought it a very doubtful advantage. But I expect I'm prejudiced.'

'Where does she live, this aunt of yours?'

'Oh Johnnie. Out there, on the Grane road.'

I knew then, of course. All I said was, 'And you don't care for her much. But you have to dance attendance. Is that it?'

'I hate her guts. Do you think we might have a drink?'

I let her hands go, but for a moment she did not move. She just stood there, staring down at me. Then she turned and for the second time went after the drinks. Her expression had not changed at all.

9

'Now tell me about your aunt,' I said.

'Are you really interested?' Claudia put her glass down, sat back at her end of the sofa and put her hands behind her head. We had come a long way since she had smiled at me with her head on one side, but the principle was the same. The apparently naïve provocativeness was not naïve at all. It was a deliberate rejection of subtlety. She knew exactly what she was doing and knew that I knew it. She could not, of course, know that with a part in my mind I was involved in a fascinated comparison between her zipped-up matt suggestiveness and the glossy detail of Daphne's *décolleté*, but so far as her own side of it went her actions were direct to the point of brutality.

I said, 'What am I supposed to say? That I'm interested in anything that concerns you? It's true, of course, so far as it goes.'

I put my glass down and got up. I refused to shuffle to her along the length of the sofa. I put my hands under her arms and stood her up. Her arms fell to her sides and stayed there while I unzipped her. I was precisely conscious of a cold undertow of apprehension, but it did not last.

I do not aim to write even polite pornography, but in view of what happened later it is to be recorded that Claudia and I became lovers, and that the experience involved a good deal of not unanticipated revelation on both sides. We were very different, but as bad as each other in some ways.

This time I poured out the drinks and we went back to our ends of the sofa. It was rather like boxers returning to their corners after an unexpectedly desperate first round.

We sat there, measuring each other up in the light of experience gained, and wondering what later rounds would be like and how we should play them. But that was only half the picture. In another part of my mind I knew that it would not take much to make me wax in Claudia's hands.

'Now tell me about your aunt,' I said. 'I know she's rich. I assume she's old. I know she lives along the Grane road. I know you shop for her and have to account for your transactions in detail. And I know you hate her guts. The picture is beginning to take shape.'

'She's my mother's sister. Her name's Barton. Elizabeth Barton. My dear Aunt Elizabeth.'

For a split second my mind checked at the name Barton and then slipped another piece of the jig-saw into place.

'I don't remember my mother. There were always the two Barton aunts, Elizabeth and Anne. Anne was the younger, and sweet. Elizabeth was always a dragon. They both had money. Anne was my godmother and was going to leave me everything, but she ran herself to death looking after Aunt Elizabeth and hadn't bothered to make a will. My father was still alive then. He wrote to Aunt Elizabeth saying he assumed Aunt Anne's money would come to me, as she had always intended. She wrote back saying that it would be unsafe to rely on intentions which Anne had never bothered to commit to writing. The money would come to her as next of kin, and my expectations, though postponed, might reasonably be expected to have been doubled. He went to see her and I expect only succeeded in putting her back up. Knowing him, he probably raved at her. When he died, I had a job and not much else. Then three years ago Aunt Elizabeth began to turn the heat on. She needed someone to look after her affairs—that was true, of course—and with my business training I was ideally suited for the job. In view of my expectations she felt I should be glad to comply with her wishes. It was a solicitor's letter—she couldn't write herself by then—and was as nicely worded a piece of legal blackmail as you could wish to see. She offered me a fixed rate of pay—it wasn't bad, actually—provided I lived in Dunstreet and placed myself at her disposal. She didn't want me in the house, thank God.'

'And you've been living here ever since?'

'Yes. Degrading, isn't it?'

'I don't know that I blame you. How long is she going to live?'

'She's in her eighties. It's not only greed, Johnnie. It's bloody-mindedness too. I ought to have had Aunt Anne's money and I'm damned well going to have it.'

'So long as you don't find she's left it all to the Cats' Home.'

'She hasn't, so far.' She spoke with complete assurance, but I did not ask her how she knew. 'But of course she's got me where she wants me, and is apt, in moments of stress, to say so. It's not very good for my character.'

I said, 'I find your character very interesting. I find everything about you interesting.'

She looked at me with that perfectly neutral concentrated stare of hers. It was not what is generally called a calculating look. It conveyed nothing whatever except the presence of an active but alien intelligence. After what had just happened I found it a little unnerving.

I said, 'I still don't quite understand why Aunt Elizabeth has to have you to help her. She's got money and she sounds more than capable of looking after herself.'

'Oh no, I suppose I didn't explain. She's blind. Completely blind now. Her sight was going all those years when Aunt Anne was killing herself for her. Now it's gone for good. But it's been so gradual, she's pretty capable in her own surroundings. Only of course she can't read or write and she can't get about much, or at any rate won't.'

78

I remembered the round pale eyes staring at me from between the crimped lace curtains of a first-floor window. I had dodged behind my rhododendron and made off like a detected burglar. And she had not even known I was there. I also remembered the long, tight-lipped smile and could see it looked blindly into Claudia's impassive stare. It was not a relationship I cared to imagine in any detail.

I said, 'She must be pretty dependent on you, if you sign papers and handle cash and so on.'

'Dependent, yes. But she doesn't trust me an inch. Not only me, of course. No one. You'd hardly believe the lengths she goes to. Anything important she won't let out of her hands once she's signed it. She seals it in specially prepared envelopes and sends it to Seaton or to the bank, so that they can check it before it goes. She's been evolving the system for years, and it's pretty well water-tight. She's quite matter-of-fact about it.'

'Who's Seaton?'

'Her solicitor. He's all right.'

'For her or for you?'

'Both. He's honest but human.'

I wondered whether Seaton's humanity extended to keeping Claudia informed on the contents of her aunt's current will. I also wondered how far his humanity extended in other directions.

'What about the envelopes?' I said. 'Does she post them herself?'

'She gives them to Coster.'

'Who in the world's Coster?'

'Her maid. Her everything. Coster's about the only person she does trust, and she's a half-wit, more or less. Wonderfully efficient, but a half-wit. It's a sweet household, what with the two old dears and Jock.'

'Who's Jock? I'm sorry if I seem a bit repetitive, but you really leave me no alternative.'

79

'That's all right. Jock's her dog. Not a proper guide dog, but they manage. I suppose you could say she trusts Jock too. That's more than I do. He's about as trustworthy as a crocodile. And I should think smells much the same, but I'm bound to say that's not his fault, poor brute. It's the life he leads. I sometimes wonder if I'm starting to smell myself.'

'I've never to my knowledge smelt a crocodile,' I said. 'But if crocodiles smell like you, I shouldn't mind keeping a couple. Tell me more about this Coster.'

'She's been there ever since I can remember. When did they stop calling superior women servants by their surnames?'

'God knows. Perhaps they still do in the sort of families that still have superior women servants. I shouldn't like to try calling my Mrs Larkin Larkin. Now you ask who's Mrs Larkin and I reply, 'My everything. She's got all her wits about her and she's marvellously inefficient." Let's leave Mrs Larkin. Why is this Coster a half-wit?'

'She's hardly even that. She hasn't got a mind of her own at all, I don't think. She's just a sort of shadow extension of Aunt Elizabeth. Only she's deaf and Aunt Elizabeth's blind. As she can't think anything without saying it and can't hear herself speak, she goes in for a sort of non-stop running commentary in a monstrous little voice that's just about audible at close range. It's like listening in on an encephalograph or something. But it's much better ignored. She's as strong as an ox and can do all the old-fashioned domestic routines with a sort of mindless perfection. Aunt Elizabeth can sometimes make her hear, as a matter of fact, but as Coster always knows in advance what she wants, she seldom needs to establish communication.'

'And you spend your days in this madhouse? How long has it been going on—three years, didn't you say?'

'Three years, all but. Johnnie, I—' I looked at her and

saw suddenly a picture of complete despair that turned my heart over. She said, 'I don't know—do you think I ought to go on? I can't get away even temporarily, do you see?'

'What would she do in fact if you went?'

'Cut me out.'

'Could you dispute it?'

'I don't think so. I'm only a niece, after all. No, either I hang on until she dies or the money goes to the Cats' Home. Dogs' Home, in fact, with special provision for Jock. Or Coster, I suppose. Coster will get something anyway, but that's fair enough.'

'When do you suppose she will die? You say she's in her eighties. Is there anything wrong with her, bar her eyes?'

'Not a thing, I don't think. She never even gets a cold, and Coster does everything for her. Bar accidents, she could live to be a hundred.'

'Accidents do happen, especially to blind old women.'

'I know. Stair rods can come loose, fires can be left unguarded, bottles can be changed. I've thought of it all. But there's always Coster—and Jock. And in any case—' She flicked her hands helplessly. 'Accidents haven't happened, and I don't really think they will.'

'No? I don't think you can be sure of that.'

We looked at each other for a bit. Then I said, 'There was one occasion, a very long time ago now, in this room. We were sitting as we are now, but quite a lot of water hadn't yet flowed under the bridge. You pointed out that we were hungry, and so we were. We went and ate lobster in one of the better residential districts of Elfhame. If I met you under the eldarn tree, could we make it again? This time I know I'm hungry without being told.' She got up and went across to the telephone.

When we were in the car I said, 'What does Mrs Pargeter do with her lobsters when we don't come?'

81

'Gives them to Mr Pargeter, I expect. He seems to keep her very happy.'

I headed the car out through the town. The street lights were already on, and I turned on my side lights. I said, 'Mr Pargeter's on an easier wicket than I am.'

She looked at me and suddenly smiled, almost for the first time that evening. 'Do your best, Johnnie. You'll find the formula yet.'

'I know the formula. It's a matter of applying it.'

She nodded. She was quite serious again.

I looked at that dark, decisive profile and wondered what I was heading for. Cartery, at one level, and a lobster supper at The Ship. At one time—it really did seem a very long time ago—I had come looking for a fabulous piece of glass and had finished at Cartery in a salt dusk with candles burning motionless in enamel candlesticks. Now I was going to Cartery again, and the thing that nagged at the back of my mind was not an enchanted cake-stand, but the sort of accident that could happen to a blind octogenarian dragon in a lost stone house.

We plunged into the tunnel of trees. I said, 'Where is this house of your aunt's? Along the Grane road, you said. I didn't see a house.'

'No? It's down a side turning. Over a bridge.'

'A bridge over what? A moat or something?

'The sea. A creek, anyway. But it goes right round. It's an island at high tide.'

So that was where the other end of the creek went. Round and back to the sea again. 'How big is this island?' I asked.

She thought. 'I don't know quite. Not big. An acre or two. It's all trees bar the house and the drive.'

'No outside work—gardens or whatnot?'

'Nothing now. I think there used to be gardens. There must have been. But it's all trees now. And nothing is ever done to them.'

82

I said, 'The woods decay, the woods decay and fall. It's funny the grip Tennyson had on primitive landscape. The Idylls of the King are all dreadful Victorians in fancy dress romping about in breath-taking early English country.'

Claudia did not turn or look at me. She stared ahead into the converging walls of trees and spoke almost in a whisper. 'Me only cruel immortality consumes. I wither slowly in thine arms.' I had not noticed how beautiful her voice was when she spoke quietly.

I put out a hand and touched her arm. She jumped and looked at me, her eyes wide open. 'Look, Claudia,' I said, 'you may do many things in my arms, but wither you won't. And no one's immortal. Tithonus didn't make a will.'

She said, 'Time's cruel enough, let alone immortality. Old age hath yet his honour and his toil. I don't think I care for Tennyson.'

The yellow lights of Cartery suddenly closed round us, and I pulled the car in to the side. 'Death closes all,' I said. I switched off the engine and lights, and found her looking at me in the phosphorescent darkness. I leant over and kissed her mouth, but it was like kissing a statue.

'I'm hungry,' she said. 'Let's go and eat.'

We ate in a bare back parlour, looking out lamp-blind across an invisible sea. Whatever it did to Mr Pargeter when we were not there, the food took over my system with the shattering efficiency of high-octane fuel. Even Claudia came alive in the lamplight. The decaying woods lost their menace and relevancy, and we made a party of it. Mrs Pargeter waited on us with the coy encouragement of the honeymoon suite, and the dram glasses came unasked after the second jug of beer.

There was something in Claudia, as there had once been in me, that was still capable of rapture, and when she gave it its head, it lit the whole place up like a naphtha flare. She was no longer the Queen of Elfhame, but a seven-year

83

indenture in her service seemed no sort of hardship. Mrs Pargeter waved goodbye from the yellow doorway, and I began to back and turn the car.

'Not the point?' said Claudia.

'Not the point. Not the high moors tonight, Claudia. There's too much running about there I don't like. Straight down under the trees and home. It's quicker and safer.'

She nodded. 'Make it quick then.'

I cannot drive fast when I am drunk, but I was not drunk, not on a couple of pints of beer and a brandy. I shot the car through the dark switchbacks with reckless and triumphant precision, and when we pulled up in Lower West Street, reality was still several miles behind.

It was much later, well after midnight, that Claudia shivered violently and said, 'I'm cold, Johnnie. Put the fire on and I'll get some tea or something.' We blinked at each other in the sudden light like strangers. The hot tea comforted us, but we had no comfort for each other.

'I must go on,' said Claudia. She stared straight into the fire and spoke almost to herself. 'There's nothing, don't you see? A job wouldn't bring in much more than now, and there'd be nothing behind it—nothing to look forward to at all, no sort of security. I can't face it.'

'Have you never thought of marrying?'

She shook her head. 'It's no good. I'm not that sort.'

'No,' I said. 'No, I don't think you are. Although at times—'

She shook her head again. 'Not you either,' she said. She got up and walked to the fireplace, leaning on the mantelpiece and looking at herself in the great gilt mirror.

'But I can't go on, Johnnie. I can't go on much longer. You've got to help me.'

'When can I see this dragon of yours?' I spoke to her back, but I felt she was watching me in the mirror.

'Tomorrow?'

'All right. Tomorrow.'

'Be on the bridge at eleven.'

'I will.' I got up and made myself ready for the road.
Even Henry had to sleep some time and there was another
man I had not seen before. I was glad of that. I wanted no
more honeymoon treatment that night. I climbed the stairs
quickly, but reality came close behind me and got into bed
before I did. The sheets were cold with it, and it was a long
time before I could get to sleep.

10

There was a lot less water in the creek than when I had first seen it. The tide was just beginning to come in slowly between flat mudbanks littered with the debris of the overhanging trees. I wondered what the bottom was like. If the mud was as soft as it looked, the place was almost as much an island at low water as it was at high.

I had left my car a quarter of a mile or more back, pulled in under the trees at the side of the road. Even with Claudia expecting me, my instinct to come stealthily was very strong. A car passing on the road above had me, almost before I knew what I was doing, half down the bank and crouched under the main timbers of the bridge. It was quite quiet here, but a slight breeze rustled in the tops of the trees and brought in the smell of the sea across the perennial background of the decaying woods.

Claudia said, 'I said on the bridge, not under it.' She must have come out on to the bridge without a sound. She leant on the side rail, looking down at me. There was a ghost of a smile on her face, but she looked pale.

'I was on it, but I heard a car.'

'Still being followed?'

'What is it, do you think, incipient persecution mania or just plain guilt?'

'What is there to feel guilty about?'

'That's for you to say. I feel like Macbeth at the end of Act One.'

She walked back across the bridge, and I scrambled up on to the road and followed her. She said over her shoulder, 'Coster's away for the morning.'

'I'm sorry. I rather wanted to see Coster.'

'Unfortunately, she might also have seen you. There's nothing wrong with her eyes.'

'Does she take herself out?'

'I take her. I drive her into town, clutching her bag of papers as if she was a King's Messenger. At least the oddity of my position doesn't seem to occur to her. She just takes it for granted. It's part of the system. There's nothing for anyone to object to.'

'And when does the King's Messenger return?'

'When I fetch her, not before. So there's only Aunt Elizabeth. And Jock, of course. But Jock isn't around all the time.'

'Has Aunt Elizabeth got all the fabulous extra senses the blind are supposed to have?'

'I've never noticed it. She was pretty old before she went blind. I should say her hearing's perfectly normal, but she won't hear you breathing, or smell you, or something, and say, "Ha! A strange man in the house!"'

'That's comforting, anyhow.' We had come to the top of the hill, and the rhododendrons closed in on both sides of us. I had last covered this stretch, in the opposite direction, at a pretty desperate run, with no very clear idea what I was running away from. I walked it now briskly, alongside Claudia, under the whispering trees, with a steadily increasing reluctance. I did not know what I was reluctant to meet any more than I had known what I wanted to get away from. I did not like the way the dark avenue sucked us into the middle of this tree-infested island. Claudia had no doubts. I suppose she was used to it.

We came round the bend of the drive on to the edge of the grey carriage-sweep. Claudia touched my arm. 'Walk over there quietly,' she said. 'Stand back against the wall by the side of the front door. When she comes out, you go in. But go quietly.'

I tiptoed across the gravel under the rows of curtained windows. I felt extraordinarily conspicuous. I stood with my back to the wall between the nearest window and the door. My mouth was dry. When I was in position, Claudia crunched firmly across the gravel to the door. A voice inside the house called, 'Claudia!'

It was not a harsh voice. It was low-pitched, absolutely assured and quite detestable. Claudia said, 'Coming, Aunt Elizabeth,' and went into the house, shutting the door behind her. I waited with my back to the wall. There was a pale sunshine filtered by drifting clouds, but even in that well of trees there was very little warmth in it. The sea must have been quite close, but there was nothing to show it was there. The trees were too thick.

I did not hear the door open, but the dog came out suddenly on to the gravel. It went straight forward away from me, with a long leather thong stretched tight behind it. I had not expected it to be attractive, but I was not prepared for anything quite so repulsive. I suppose it was some sort of bull-terrier. It was pinky-white all over, and looked quite naked and scrofulous. Even from sideways its eyes were almost invisible between the puckered pink lids. It waddled and wheezed like a fat dog, but you could see most of the bones under the hanging skin. Its smell went past me as it walked. On the end of the lead came a long black glove and behind it Claudia's Aunt Elizabeth.

I had had no idea, seeing her through a curtained window like that, how tall she was. She must have been all of six foot, and her elaborately coiled hair put as much on her height as a policeman's helmet. She was scrupulously tidy and completely monochrome, as if the colour had drained out of her with her failing eyesight. Only her gloves were dead black. I had somehow expected rustling silks, but she wore heavy tweeds and brogues. Her feet were as big as the rest of her. Her back was ramrod straight, but the whole body bent forward a bit to the pull of the waddling dog. She walked briskly and without hesitation. Claudia had said she could live to be a hundred. She looked to me as if, left to herself, she would live for ever. The skin was grey but clear and glossy, and her smile, as she passed me, came back almost under her ear.

The pair of them walked straight out across the gravel sweep away from me. They were almost at the far side when I realised that they would turn, one way or the other, when they got there, and that the dog at least might see me. Then I remembered what Claudia had said. I took two quick but cautious steps and went in at the door. The whole place smelt of the dog.

Claudia stood behind the open door, waiting for me. 'You were right about one thing,' I said. 'Your aunt won't smell me, not in this house. At least, I hope not.'

'I told you. Crocodile.' We were talking in whispers.

'How long will they be out there?'

'A quarter of an hour or more. It's their exercise.'

I went to the door cautiously and looked out. Round and round the edge of the grey gravel sweep the pink scraggy dog panted steadily at the end of the leash, and its mistress, unhurried but bent always slightly forward, marched behind. Her flat shoes crunched on the gravel, and the dog wheezed in an uneasy rhythm that matched their beat.

Claudia, behind me, said, 'Come on. I'll show you the house. The door stays open. I don't think they'll come in unexpectedly, but in any case there are two back doors. And back stairs.' The crunching and wheezing grew loud suddenly, and the dog and the huge woman went past the door, within a few feet of us. Neither looked at us. Their close-lipped grins were very much alike.

I said, 'It's not people who get like their dogs. It's the other way round. I've always thought so, and this proves it. She can't be copying the dog. Or could she see it once?'

'It's difficult to remember. It's not as old as it looks, but it's been here some time. Yes, I should think she must have seen it pretty clearly before her eyes really packed up. But I'm sure you're right. That expression is all Aunt Elizabeth. It always was, long before Jock's time. Anyhow, dogs see much more than we do. This is the dining-room.'

'Still used?'

'Oh yes—the whole house is used exactly as it was before she went blind. I told you—it happened so gradually. There was no sudden adaptation to changed circumstances. In any case, Aunt Elizabeth doesn't adapt herself, suddenly or otherwise. Everything else adapts itself to her.'

The rooms and almost everything in them were Victorian, early Victorian at most. I remembered the bank manager saying the Bartons had been there three hundred years, and wondered. I said, 'None of this is very old. I'd expected something more ancestral. How long has the family lived here?'

'Generations. Well—several hundred years, anyhow. But the old house was burnt. This was built—well, you can see. Eighteen-fortyish, I suppose.'

'Was all the stuff lost with the house?'

'Most of it, but they got the treasures out, or what they thought of then as the treasures. Pictures, mostly, and some silver. It's all upstairs in Aunt Elizabeth's rooms.'

'Does that all smell the same?'

'Worse. The dog sleeps at the back, actually—in the house, but at the back, by the scullery. But it's upstairs most of the day.'

'You said you didn't trust it. What is its reaction to strangers, in fact? If your aunt's sitting in that chair with this horror at her feet and I walk in at the door, so quietly that she doesn't know I'm there—what does it do? Attack me, or bark, or what?'

'I'm not sure. I've never seen it happen. I'd say it would stop wheezing and look at you without saying a word. Then if you came nearer, the wheeze would turn to a growl. Ultimately, I suppose, if you came right up without speaking, it would get up and snarl. It's never done more than growl at me. It's pretty apathetic, poor brute. But of course, she'd be saying, "Who's there?" as soon as it stopped wheezing almost. I told you, she's got nothing special in the way of hearing herself, but the dog certainly acts as a sort of radar station for her, apart from actually leading her round things.'

We looked at each other in that cluttered, dog-filled dining-room. 'They're a sweet pair, aren't they?' I said. She was staring at me with her blank, distant stare. She said, 'You've never hated anyone, have you, Johnnie? Not consistently, day in, day out, I mean. You wouldn't be bothered.'

'Not like that, except one or two of my schoolmasters, and that's all some time ago. I go in more for the short-term stuff.'

'Yes. I shouldn't like to be on your short-term list, I don't think.'

I shook my head at her. 'I never do anything,' I said. We were both perfectly serious.

'No? There's always a first time. Are they still on the march?'

I looked out between the draped muslin curtains. The procession went on. I said, 'Don't they ever go anywhere else?'

'Not her. The dog goes out on its own occasionally, of course. But that's from the back. And not far. Come and see upstairs.'

The stairs were painted wood, as solid as brickwork, but steep and not particularly wide. A thick red carpet was laid down the middle under brass rods. The eyes were spiked

91

home into the woodwork, with the rods standing inches clear on each side. There were no fancy modern latches. With the pressure of that carpet under them, you would need a hammer to shift the rods sideways out of the eyes. There was no room for accident there.

'You see?' said Claudia. I nodded. 'Here's her sitting-room.'

It was a monochrome room, all faded carpets and upholstery and bleached panelling. The family portraits saved from the fire did not get above the level of interesting archives. They were not worth anything. There were some shelves of books which were presumably never read. I saw no silver or glass anywhere. There was a big upright arm-chair, moulded exactly to the shape of that huge immobil-ised body, with a stained rug at its foot. The whole room was perfectly clean but smelt terrible. On one side of the fireplace, almost behind the chair, a flat blank section in the panelling looked like a wall-cupboard. I thought there was a keyhole, but could not be certain without looking closer. It was much too big for a modern wall-safe, but might still be very strong. There was a table by the chair, littered with stuff that groping hands, however practised, could not keep tidy. It included bottles and glasses, and there was a jug of some pale liquid under a white muslin cover weighted down with blue glass beads.

'Where does she sleep?' I asked. 'Through there?' I nodded towards the farther door.

'Yes, that's it. There's not much.' She walked over and opened the door. I went to the window and looked out. Immediately in front of me and, with the slope of the ground, not far below me was the last rhododenron bush. This was where the round, pale eyes had watched from, seeing nothing. No one lurked in the rhododendrons now, but as I looked the two fantastic figures, still linked by the leather thong, marched steadily across my field of vision

92

and vanished again. 'They're still at it,' I said.

I walked across to the open door and looked through into the bedroom. The smell was noticeably less here. Jock slept downstairs. There was a very large, almost square iron bedstead with brass knobs on the posts. The table beside it, like the one in the other room, was littered with stuff. The furniture here was standard mid-Victorian, but the dressing-table had no mirror. There were more pictures, of no greater interest, but nothing approaching ornaments. There was what looked like a trunk under the massive bed, but no wall-cupboard I could see. We came back into the sitting-room, and Claudia shut the connecting door.

As we reached the landing door, Claudia put a hand on my arm. I stopped and looked at her. Then the front door banged heavily below us, and that quiet, wicked voice said, 'Claudia?'

She said, 'Yes, Aunt Elizabeth?' and pointed along to the far end of the landing. I nodded and went off on tiptoe.

'What are you doing upstairs?'

'Tidying, Aunt Elizabeth.' She walked to the head of the stairs as I found, further along, the dark well of the back staircase.

'Tidying.' The voice was quite expressionless. It asked no question and offered no comment. 'I thing it is time you fetched Coster.'

'Very well, Aunt Elizabeth.' We began, simultaneously, the descent of our respective staircases. I got to the bottom of mine and stood listening. The front door banged again. I thought Claudia must have gone out, but I did not know where her car was. Not a stair creaked over my head, but I heard, faint but unmistakable, a steady wheeze and rustle as Jock guided his mistress upstairs.

I was in a dark passage. The smell of dog from the back of the house was very strong. I went to the end of the passage and through an open door. It was some sort of

93

back kitchen, and a cubby-hole on my left was unmistakably where Jock slept. There was also, I noticed, a chain stapled to the wall and a drinking bowl full of water. I tiptoed through the kitchen towards what ought to be the back door of the house. I put my hand on the handle and stopped dead. The wheezing, moving quicker this time, came down the main stairs into the hall and along the passage towards me. Without taking my hand off the door I turned my head and watched.

Across the doorway behind me the pink creature waddled to its den. It looked neither right nor left. It lapped steadily at the water in the bowl, stood stock-still for a moment and then turned and waddled back along the passage. As it started to climb the stairs, I opened the door, went out and shut it quietly behind me. For all the rotten smell of the woods, the clean air struck with almost painful sweetness at the back of my nostrils. For a moment or two I breathed deeply, trying to get rid of the rising nausea that took me suddenly by the throat. Then my head cleared, and I made my way round the farther end of the house.

I was too late. As I rounded the corner, Claudia's green Morris turned off the carriage-sweep and roared away up the drive in second gear. The sound was muffled by the rhododendrons, but I heard the note drop as she reached the top of the hill and turned down through the trees towards the bridge. I knew why she had not waited. I had no doubt Aunt Elizabeth was listening too. I imagined her, bolt upright in the tall chair with the stinking creature at her feet, listening with her thin smile while another of her creatures went off to fetch the third. There was nothing more I needed to know. All I had to do was to be out of the way, or at least out of sight, by the time Claudia came back with Coster.

I walked very quietly across the gravel. It is curious how difficult it is to persuade oneself of the fact of another person's blindness. I made no sound, and therefore for Aunt Elizabeth did not exist. But I was conscious at every step of the overlooking windows, and if I had seen, as I had before, the round eyes watching me from upstairs, I should have been hard put to it not to run.

In fact, I saw nothing. I reached the end of the rhododendrons, turned in behind them with illogical relief and began to walk up the drive. Half-way up I checked, hesitated and turned back. I did not know how long Claudia would be, but I did not want to go just yet.

11

I turned my back on the house, crossed the drive and plunged straight down the bank on the far side. It was heavy going, but not impenetrable. The trees were too closely grown to allow any real thicket under them. There was a lot of fallen wood, branches and whole stems leaning at all angles, and the ground itself was unreliable. It crumbled underfoot and was heavily mined by the various burrowing creatures that lived wild and undisturbed in the wood. Almost at once I saw the shine of water at the foot of the slope. The tide should be well up now.

I came out on to the bank of the creek at a point that seemed to be a couple of hundred yards seaward of the bridge. There was clear water now almost to the roots of the trees on each side. The far bank went up steeply to the horizontal fold in the trees that marked the line of the road. I worked my way along to the right until I could just see the mainland abutments of the bridge. Then I turned and went back, working my way round the edge of the island just inside the trees.

The southern tip projected into a broad creek of open water which split and passed on each side of it. The whole thing must be pear-shaped. At some point the sea had worked its way round behind the high ground at its northern end and cut it off from the mainland. I imagine the process was continuing and the whole island gradually eroding away. There did not seem to be any land-water bringing down enough silt to counteract it. I went on slowly up the eastern side of the pear. The far bank sloped more gently here, but I could see no sign of any road on that side. The

96

country stretched away in fields and wooded valleys, presumably until it climbed the high ground above Cartery Point.

The shore took on a pronounced left-handed curve, and I knew I was getting near the northern end. It could not be all that big. Claudia's one or two acres would be about right, but I did not think it could be as much as two.

At the northern end, where the shore ran in a flat east-west curve, the creek looked much shallower and there was more mud still showing on either side. I did not know when high tide was, but it looked as if it had another six inches to make. Then I stopped dead.

Straight across me, leading down out of the trees to the edge of the creek, there was a clear and startlingly fresh track of human feet. I do not pretend to be an expert in these matters, but I could not believe that the track was more than a few hours old. I followed it to the water's edge, and that clinched it. The tide was even now creeping over, and obliterating, the footprints that went down over the near mud and disappeared under the water. Whoever it was had walked down the bank and, apparently, across the creek while the tide was out. He had walked barefoot. I pictured a man walking gingerly on soft mud and probably carrying his shoes. Not being, as I say, an expert, I could not swear to the sex, but the feet were certainly fairly large, though probably smaller than mine. I thought I saw, but could not swear to, a couple of prints leading up on the far side, but the branches hung low over the water there, and it was impossible to be certain.

I worked my way round the northern end till I came to the bridge, but found no more tracks, coming or going. Unless the unknown had crossed the creek close to the bridge on its other side, where I had not explored in detail, he must have come in over the bridge. The other alternative seemed unlikely. Assuming that his purpose was secrecy,

97

I could not see him wading across the creek at a point where he himself, and his tracks behind him, would be in full view of the bridge.

I turned and climbed straight up through the trees to the higher ground above the back of the house. Whatever the tracks meant, they laid my guilt complex and my persecution mania abruptly to rest. There was someone about.

I skirted round the curve at the top of the drive and came down the green bank behind the house. If the car had come back, I should have heard it. There could be no one watching from the back windows, or no one who had eyes to see me with. So long as I was quiet, I was not there. I went very quietly indeed.

I was half-way down the bank when the noise started inside the house. I think, even now, it was the most horrible noise I have ever heard. It was a series of short, sharp jabbing screams, as if someone was yanking and letting go the pull of a siren with a good head of steam under it. The screams were high-pitched but throaty. I could not easily associate them with the low-pitched, decisive voice of Aunt Elizabeth, but she was the only person in the house.

I stood where I was for a second or two while the screaming went on inside. I had no doubt whatever that Aunt Elizabeth was better dead, but I found it in practice absolutely impossible to stand there and let her scream. The screaming itself was intolerable. I started to scramble down the bank, stumbled, came down almost head first, recovered myself and got down to the back door. Then the screams stopped.

I opened the door, quietly this time, went in and shut it behind me. It was surprisingly dark inside and the smell hit me at once. I took two steps and trod on something soft and flatulent spreadeagled across the stone floor. It was quite inert. I staggered sideways and got my hand on a wall. A wave of the most appalling nausea swept over me.

I bowed my head across my arm and shut my eyes, trying desperately not to vomit where I stood. As my senses cleared a little, I heard a car drive crunching over the gravel and stop outside the front door. Then, very close at hand now, the screaming started again.

I turned and made for the door. I tried not to look at what was on the floor, but I knew perfectly well what it was. I got outside the door and shut it behind me.

Then I heard feet running towards me round the end of the house. I dodged inside the open door of what looked like a coal-shed, but turned out to be an outside lavatory. The steps ran up to the back door, and I heard the old-fashioned swish of long skirts and the high thin continuous murmur of sound I had heard the first day I came. The only words I heard were, 'The saucer. Oh please God it is not the saucer. Not the saucer.' Then the door slammed shut and the voice stopped. I stood there, with my head against the whitewashed brickwork of the lavatory wall, while the horror seeped slowly out of me and I started to think.

Two things, at any rate, were apparent. Claudia and Coster were back, and Aunt Elizabeth, for better or worse, was not dead, whatever else was. There did not seem to be anything I had to do, and with Coster around there was not much I could. I came out of my dank hiding place and ran quickly along the back of the house to the far end. With seeing eyes in the back windows, the clear bank behind the house was not for me. I dodged across a bit of gravel, turned in behind what was probably the garage and took to the shelter of the trees. Once there and out of sight of the house, I began to work my way steadily round northwards to the far side of the high ground and, ultimately, the bridge. The tide must be right up now, and in any case I did not want to leave another set of tracks in the mud, even for the pleasure of comparing my bare footprints with those of the unknown.

I reached the bridge, listened, heard nothing and walked across it. I saw and heard nothing on the road until I reached my car. I wondered whether Claudia knew where I had left it and whether she had seen it there when she returned with Coster. It was well screened from the road, but not, of course, invisible if you knew where to look. I backed the car out and drove into Dunstreet. It was well past lunch-time, and in any case I did not feel hungry.

When I got in, Henry had a message for me. 'Miss James phoned,' he said. 'She asked if you were in, and I said I hadn't seen you. She said would you ring her at four.' He gave me the number. It was the number of the Lower West Street flat. I thanked him and went upstairs.

Claudia must have been waiting for the call. She picked up the receiver the moment I rang and said, 'Johnnie? What happened to you?'

'I tried to catch you before you went,' I said, 'but I was too late. I stayed about. I hoped to see you when you came back. I was still there when you came. What happened to Aunt Elizabeth? She was screaming blue murder—just before you came and just after. I didn't know whether to go in or not at first. Then I thought I must. I was just going in when you came. Then as Coster was presumably around I thought I'd better go. Is she all right? Aunt Elizabeth, I mean.'

'She's all right, yes.'

'Then what was it all about?'

She hesitated. Then she said, 'Can you meet me somewhere?'

'When?'

'Now.'

'Can't I come round?'

100

'No. No, I don't think—Look, meet me at the Cartery turning in about ten minutes. All right?'

I said, 'Whatever you say.' I was there before her. I turned into the side road, pulled the car as far in to the bank as it would go, got out and walked back to the turning. She pulled up by me a minute later. 'Where's your car?' she said. 'Down the lane?'

I nodded. 'It will be all right for a bit. Shall I get in?'

'No, don't do that. I'm taking the road to the point— you know, left between here and the Grane turning. Will you follow? I'll wait for you somewhere.'

She hardly looked at me. She was staring straight in front of her, but whether she was watching the road ahead, or her driving mirror, or both, I could not be sure. I said, 'All right,' and went back to my car. The moment I left her she was off, and by the time I had backed in the lane and got back to the main road there was no sign of her.

I took the next turning left, and the road began to climb, never steeply, but steadily. I had not come this way before by daylight. As I thought, it was moorland, fairly flat once you were up on to it, and with nothing to see anywhere except heather and occasional birch scrub. Away to the west, beyond the valley where the Grane road ran out to the sea, there was a long ridge of even higher ground, broken at two places by the derelict mine-workings I had noticed during my first exploration round Dunstreet.

I saw Claudia first as a distant figure by the roadside. She looked tiny in that edgeless landscape. Even when I got closer, I still could not see the Morris. She signalled me down a track to the right and I turned obediently into it. It dived into what looked like a shallow quarry, not more than twenty or thirty yards across. The walls were cut rock, but nowhere more than ten feet high. At the bottom was a flat green stretch with the Morris standing in the middle of

101

it. I drove past Claudia and parked alongside. Then I got
out and walked back to meet her.

I said, 'Now who's being followed? Or is it just persecution with you too?'

She ignored this. She looked at me directly for the first
time since I had met her at the Cartery turning. She said,
'How long were you in the house after I left?'

'No time at all. It's not a house I'd choose to linger in. I
found a back door and got out.'

'Which way did you go?'

'Round to the far end of the house. I didn't know where
your car was, but I hoped to find you before you went.'

'No—I mean inside the house.'

'Inside? I went down the back stairs when you went
down the front. I came out in a sort of passage. I went to
the end of it and through an open door. It was a scullery or
something. There was a back door of the house to the
right.'

'Did you see Jock?'

'Yes. Just before I went out. I saw his chain and bowl to
the left as I went into the scullery place. I was just going
out when he appeared in person. He didn't see me, luckily.'

'What did he do, then?'

'Had a drink of water, presumably from his bowl, and
went back upstairs.'

'How long was that before Aunt Elizabeth started screaming?'

'Oh, some time. Well, obviously—long enough for you
to pick up Coster and get back.'

'Where were you all that time?'

'In the wood, exploring. But never far from the house.'

'You didn't see Jock again during that time?'

'No, he was upstairs with your aunt, I imagine.'

She nodded. 'Now tell me what's happened,' I said.

'Someone's poisoned Jock. He's dead.'

102

'I can't say I'm sorry. He can't have got much fun out of life, and he was a pain in the neck to everyone else. Except Aunt Elizabeth, I suppose.'

'Except Aunt Elizabeth, yes.'

'Hence the screams. What happened?'

'The dog was up with her apparently. I suppose the stuff started to work. She could hear the dog threshing about and gasping, but, of course, she couldn't see anything. I think—I honestly don't believe her blindness has ever really hit her before. That must have been when she started to scream. Then the poor brute ran downstairs. I suppose it was trying to get out or something. Anyhow, it collapsed in the scullery. It was quite dead when we got back. Aunt Elizabeth went downstairs after it, but slowly, of course. She was just in the passage leading to the scullery when she heard my car at the front door. Then she started to scream again. I came in through the hall and found her. Coster had gone round the end of the house, and she came running in at the back. That was all there was—the dog dead in the scullery and Aunt Elizabeth screaming in the passage. Where were you?'

'Out at the back, out of sight but within earshot.'

'You didn't see anyone anywhere?'

'No. Are you sure the dog was poisoned?'

'Pretty certain, yes. There was a good deal of froth and mess.'

'It could have been a fit. God knows it looked unhealthy enough. And smelt it.'

'I know, but I don't think so.'

'You could get a vet to do a post-mortem.'

'I could, yes. I'm not sure—'

'What about Aunt Elizabeth? What does she think?'

'I've told her Jock had a fit.'

'And what about Coster?'

'I don't know what Coster thinks. I never do. I told you

103

—I'm not even sure she thinks at all. But if Aunt Elizabeth says a fit, a fit it will be.'

'But you think it was poisoned? By whom? You didn't poison it yourself?'

We looked at each other, standing there between the parked cars in that curious green amphitheatre hidden from everything in the middle of nowhere. Claudia's face was as blank as I had ever seen it, but there was a mind behind it. The mind was thinking hard, but I did not know what. Finally she shook her head. 'I didn't poison the dog,' she said. 'Did you?'

I shook my head in turn. 'I repeat—I'm not sorry it's dead. But think. I'd never seen it before this morning. I admit that to see it was to desire its death. Come to that, the same applies to your Aunt Elizabeth. But I don't carry poison about with me on the chance. If I had, I'd have been more inclined to pop it in Aunt Elizabeth's jug with the blue glass beads than into Jock's drinking bowl. Of course, it could be a sort of step in the right direction, I suppose. But I didn't, in fact, do it. I'm not at all sure I could, but of course you've only my word for that.'

She still stood there looking at me. She said, 'You don't like dead dogs, do you, Johnnie? Or dead deer, or dead anything. But you might, as you say, desire their death. I should have thought poison was just your cup of tea.'

I smiled at her. 'We've got far beyond the possibility of insulting each other,' I said. 'Insult apart, I think your choice of phrase unfortunate.'

She smiled back at me, almost gaily. 'No insult intended, Johnnie. I only wanted to know.'

'You know as much as I do,' I said.

She was still smiling. She said, 'More, probably.' We left it at that.

104

12

I saw nothing of Claudia for nearly forty-eight hours after that, and there was very little I could do about it. I phoned her flat at pretty regular intervals, but got no reply. I even loitered discreetly in Lower West Street, but never saw her come or go. I could not try to get hold of her at the Barton house. Coster was not blind and Aunt Elizabeth was not deaf. And the telephone was on the littered table alongside her armchair.

To say that I was worried is really quite inadequate. I was in a perpetual ferment of anxiety and doubt. I did not like barefoot tracks in the mud and dead dogs. I did not mind Jock's being dead. In almost any other circumstances I should have jumped at it. But someone seemed to have poisoned him, and I did not think it was Claudia and I knew it was not me. As I say, I did not mind his being dead, but I did not like someone else's wanting him out of the way and getting him out. And I did not like Claudia's playing hide-and-seek in deserted quarries. For the first time I felt that time was not on my side, and for the first time I could do very little to force the pace. And I wanted to see Claudia. I did not think very clearly about this, but I wanted to see her very badly indeed.

By the afternoon of the second day I had to do something. I put my car well away from the Grane road and walked on towards the turning by the bridge. You could not see far on either side of the road, but there was little solid cover close to it. Twice I heard cars and had to run well into the trees and throw myself flat on the damp leaves. Both times I heard the car go past but never saw it. Well before I got to the turning I veered off left-handed at a slight angle to the road and made my way cautiously through the wood. In fact I did not have to go very far before I found what I was looking for. There was a small clearing in the trees to the left of the road and well below it, with a track of sorts you could run a car down. You could not see it from the road. If I had seen it, I should almost certainly have left my car there instead of further back on the other side. Someone had done his reconnaissance better than I had, and he had done just that. I am not an Australian aborigine or even a Second-Class Scout, but there was no mistaking the car tracks in the soft stuff underfoot. That, to the ordinary man like myself, was about all there was to see. A car had gone down the track to the clearing, stopped there and backed out again on to the road without trying to turn. It had probably done it more than once. I did not know when it had done it, or how often, or what sort of a car it was, or even what sort of tyres it had.

But I knew what someone had done when he had stopped the car in the clearing. I knew that because I already knew the other end of the story. He had got out and walked down through the wood to the bridge. Later he had come back to the car from the creek at a point opposite the northern end of the island. As with the car, there was nothing very clear or identifiable, but the track was there. There was a line of disturbance through the wood. Someone had walked up through it, pushing things aside and flattening things down. In fact, I lost the track before I reached the water, but I knew pretty well where it was leading. I made my way down towards the creek, always under cover of the trees and always, for no very good reason I could give myself, going as quietly as I could. There was next to no wind and no sound anywhere but a gentle rustle in the leaves overhead.

In fact, I heard the noise almost as soon as I saw the

106

water. It was a watery noise, a gentle repetitive swashing, as if someone was dabbling a hand in the shallow water under the trees. It came from a bit over to my left. I went towards it, as quickly and quietly as I could, until I could see the water between the trees all along my side. There was nothing there. Whatever was making the noise was making it on the far side. I crept down towards the water, crouching and peering under the hanging branches, with my view extending further and further across the creek.

Very soon after that the sound stopped, but for a second or two before it stopped I saw what was making it. It was a stick, quite a long stick, reaching down to the edge of the water from under the shelter of the trees. I got a glimpse, but no more than a glimpse, of a hand holding the other end of it, but I could have guessed the hand without seeing it, and I saw nothing more. The stick was dabbling about at the water's edge, splashing the water systematically over a patch of mud which the tide had not reached. Unless I was very much mistaken, it was obliterating, very carefully but forty-eight hours too late, the tracks I had seen leading into the water on the far side.

It was quite quiet now. The stick had stopped sloshing the water over the mud and been pulled up under the branches. I tried to hear, but could not, the sound of some-body moving back up the bank on the far side. I started to move back myself, but before I moved back I took a long look at the mud on my side of the creek. I saw what I expected to see. No tracks, but an uneven puddled patch where, on the narrow lip of mud between the fallen leaves and the edge of the water, the tracks had emerged on my side.

As I got farther from the creek, I sacrificed silence increasingly to speed. I did not bother to get back to the road, but made direct across the long slope towards the mainland end of the bridge. I came out, in fact, slightly above it, but moved down to it under cover of the trees. Then I stopped and listened. There was still nothing to hear anywhere but the faint steady rustling of the wind in the tops of the trees. I stepped out cautiously on to the edge of the road, but could see nothing. I crossed the bridge, walked half-way up the steep length of drive on the far side and turned off left-handed into the trees. Almost at once I heard something moving, and stopped dead. The sound came from over on my right, close to the bend of the drive where the rhododendrons started. A second later I heard someone walking down the drive towards the bridge. I turned to face the drive and waited.

She walked steadily down the drive within a few yards of me. Her head was up, her mouth tight shut, her pace regular. There was nothing stealthy about her at all. I said, 'Claudia!' and went out on to the drive.

She had stopped and was walking back towards me. She said 'Johnnie! What are you doing lurking in the woods?'

'Looking for you,' I said. 'I wondered what had happened to you.'

'I've been busy.'

'About Jock?'

'Jock? Not particularly, no.'

'But what's happened about that?'

'Nothing's happened, I don't think. The dog's dead and buried.'

'Buried? Who buried it? Not you?'

'Not me, no. Coster, of course. Well, someone had to. It's two days since it died. Or did you think we'd just throw it in the creek?'

I had not thought about it at all, of course, not as a problem of disposal. I said, 'Did you get an examination done?'

She shook her head. 'What good would that do? Aunt Elizabeth assumes a fit.'

108

'And what do you assume?'

'I don't assume anything. I didn't poison it, and you say you didn't. For all I know it may have been a fit. There's no other obvious explanation.' She was not defiant or argumentative. She was just not particularly interested, as if she could not see what all the fuss was about.

I said, 'How's Aunt Elizabeth getting on without the dog?'

She shrugged slightly. 'As you might suppose. Very competently. She didn't need it half the time. And for the other half she manages.'

'What about her exercise?'

'Coster's rigged up an enclosure for her. A sort of geriatric playpen. She uses a stick and goes round and round inside it. She's at it now.'

'Hasn't she used a stick before?'

'No. That's come in as a substitute for the dog.'

'An ebony cane with a carved ivory handle—that sort of thing?'

'Not that sort of thing at all. You've seen her, haven't you? Ashplant, almost as thick as my wrist. She could knock you down with it. Only of course she wouldn't know where to hit.'

I started to walk up the drive towards the house. She hesitated and then came after me. 'Where are you going?' she said.

'I want to see these new excitements—the ashplant and the geriatric playpen, particularly. Where's Coster?'

'Coster's out.'

'Then don't let me keep you, if you have other business on hand.' Her shoes were perfectly clean, but then the soft stuff under foot in the wood would not have dirtied them. There was no mud on her hands or clothes. She was still walking beside me, but still doubtfully. I said, 'How's the persecution complex? Still in hot pursuit?'

'No one's pursuing me, Johnnie. Nor you either, so far as I've seen.'

'Except each other, of course.'

'Are we pursuing each other?'

'Aren't we? I've spent two days trying to catch up with you, and at the moment you seem to be following me pretty closely.' I stopped suddenly and caught hold of her hands. I pulled her to me. She came without any trace of resistance, but still as if she did not know what all the fuss was about. I said, 'What's come over you, Claudia? You've withdrawn to a vast distance. So vast that I know I've no hope of reaching you, only I don't seem to stop trying. It's ever since that filthy dog died. But I can't see what difference that makes. You don't seem to think it very important yourself.' I kissed her.

She kissed me back and said, 'The dog? No, I don't think that's important at all.'

I let go her hands and we went on walking towards the house. We said nothing for a long time. This was as well, because when we turned the bend of the drive to go down towards the front of the house, we found Aunt Elizabeth standing in front of us.

She was still wearing her tweeds and massive shoes, but this time she had no gloves on. Her hands were the only graceful thing about her, curiously small on that massive body, but they held on to the rough stick with obvious and incongruous strength. I stood still, wondering whether Claudia and I had really, as I thought, been walking in step. Claudia walked on towards her.

'Claudia?'

'Yes, Aunt Elizabeth?'

'Where have you been? I thought I heard voices at the far end of the drive.'

'I don't think you can have. I have just come from there.

110

Unless I have started talking to myself, like Coster. That seems just possible.'

'You think similar pressures are likely to produce similar symptoms—even in what must, I think, be regarded as widely differing subjects?' The round grey eyes looked just over Claudia's shoulder and, disconcertingly, straight at me. The effect was very owl-like. Not the wise old owl of children's stories, but the creature the mouse sees. If I could have thought of any way, any way at all, of beating her head in where she stood and getting away with it, I should not have hesitated for a moment.

Claudia stood with her hands behind her back and her feet straddled and looked at her aunt. She even had her head a little on one side. She said, 'It's a question of time partly, don't you think? There must have been a lot of native strength in Coster, I should imagine. It was never there in my time, of course.'

'Coster knows when she's well placed.' She never raised her voice or stopped smiling her close-lipped smile, but her brows contracted between the sightless, staring eyes, and her hands worked convulsively on the stick. The blind fury, I thought. The blind fury with the abhorred shears. I could not remember where the phrase came from, but this huge colourless creature filled me with an almost incredulous horror. She said, 'Whether or not you are is entirely for you to decide.'

'I have decided,' Claudia said. 'I know exactly how I am placed.'

The old woman said nothing. Then she shifted her stick to her right hand and reached out suddenly with her left. For a moment my mind struggled with itself. Then it had what it wanted. I hardly dared to breathe, but my heart beat so heavily that I thought it must be audible at half-a-dozen paces.

Aunt Elizabeth said, 'Come here, Claudia.' Claudia

111

moved towards her, and the hand touched and settled on her shoulder, gripping it with that same unexpected strength. 'Walk down the drive, please, and let me keep a hand on you. I don't like walking alone when there are people about.'

'There are no people about, Aunt Elizabeth. I don't know why you should think there are.'

'No? Not now, perhaps. But there have been lately. I don't like it. I don't like it, do you hear?' She yanked suddenly at Claudia's shoulder, and Claudia, who was no lightweight, spun around against her and bounced off with the immediate, instinctive revulsion of the cat which lands on something it does not like.

She walked off steadily down the drive, with her aunt holding her but not leaning on her. She said, 'I know you don't like people here, Aunt Elizabeth. You never have, have you? But there aren't any. Only me and Coster.'

I let them go perhaps ten yards and then began to follow, stepping very cautiously. When I got to the last rhododendron, they were half-way across the gravel, and I stopped. Coster had driven a ring of posts, only a couple of feet high but very solid, into the gravel and linked them with wire. The only gap was opposite the front door and perhaps four yards from it. It was all perfectly efficient but somehow sub-human. As I watched, Aunt Elizabeth touched the wire with her stick. She took her hand off Claudia and made her way briskly round the outside of the ring towards the front door. When she got to the gap she turned and went inside. Claudia followed her in. I stayed where I was, looking up at the house. I had it all now. I should have had it before if it had not been for the gloves.

The first I had seen of Claudia's Aunt Elizabeth, apart from the unidentified face at the first floor window, had been that gloved left hand, holding one end of the leash that dragged her forward after the panting dog. Now the

112

glove was off, and I had seen the hand itself. There had been that split second of displacement, as when one sees what one has up to now seen only in dreams, and then I had identified, quite rationally, the square-cut ruby with the chased work round it and the triple branching ring. I had, of course, seen Aunt Elizabeth's hands before. They were in the negatives of old Levinson's photographs. They had been holding, with that obsessive pressure I now recognised as characteristic, the Verzelini tazza.

It was upstairs, in the wall-cupboard in the sitting-room. I did not know why she kept it like that, or how much she knew about it, or in what circumstances she had allowed Levinson to photograph it. But I knew she had it, and I knew she never let anyone else touch it. On reflection, I did not really know that she kept it in the wall-cupboard, but that was where I thought it was.

Claudia came out of the front door and walked round to the far end of the house, where she kept her car. I started to walk up the drive, and before I reached the top of the rise heard the Morris coming up after me. I stood at the side and waved her down.

'Going to fetch Coster?' I said.

She nodded. Her face was absolutely blank again.

'My car's half-a-mile along the road. May I come that far?'

She nodded again, and I got in beside her. As the car turned out on to the road I said, 'You're quite right, it can't go on.'

'It's not.' She spoke in a perfectly matter-of-fact voice.

I looked at her but said nothing. She said, 'Apart from anything else, I don't think Aunt Elizabeth will let it. You heard her.'

'Just here,' I said. 'The car's off the road a bit.' She stopped the Morris and I got out. I went round to her side and stood looking down at her. She gave me one quick upward glance. She said, 'Time's running out, Johnnie. I'm no longer worried about immortality.'

I did not know what to say. While I was thinking, the car moved off.

13

I did not think for very long. I knew, at least, what to do, and I reckoned I had time to do it before Claudia and Coster brought two pairs of working eyes back to the house. I ran the car out of the trees and drove hard to the bridge. This time I did not bother to hide the car. I left it where I had left it the first time. I ran down over the bridge, walked up the steep slope because I did not feel up to running, and then jog-trotted, as quietly as I could, but at a pretty steady pace, down the long avenue between the rhododendrons.

When I came to the gravel sweep, I looked up at the front of the house. The windows were blind, and I walked on, very quietly now, making for the far end of the house. Half-way across I looked up again, and all my commonsense could not keep my legs moving. There was the round-eyed face where I had seen it the first time, staring out at me. But not at me, I kept on saying, not at me. Whatever was going on in that stifled furious head, it was not thinking of me. It did not know I existed, let alone that I was mincing across the gravel ten feet below it and as many yards to the front.

I got my legs moving again and then stopped. She had dropped her face now and was staring down. I could see her hands moving. Under the cover of the draped muslin and the stone sill she was turning something round and round in her hands. I could not see it any more than she could, but I could not miss the bending, passionate concentration of the bowed head. The smile was still there, but for the first time the lips were parted. It was horrible, but I knew what it was. It was the smile of the madonna playing with the baby in her lap. I swallowed on a dry mouth and hurried on to the window I had in mind.

None of these ground-floor windows was ever opened, and they were all permanently latched. I pulled my knife out and then thought I was only making things hard for myself. I put it back and tiptoed to the front door. I waited, listening, but heard nothing. The door opened quietly and I put my head in. The smell of dog was fading already, but I did not think it would ever disappear, and staleness lent it a fresh horror. I left the door standing ajar, turned right and walked into the dining-room.

The window at the far end was latched and, as I thought, the latch had been in position for a long time. I wrapped my handkerchief round it and wrestled with it. I did not think I was making too much noise. Finally it gave. I eased it back until it was fully open, put my hands under the hooks on the bottom of the sash and pulled. Just for a moment something, probably the paint between sash and sill, stuck. Then it let go with a gentle crack, and the big sash rolled up with commendable silence.

That was all I wanted. I pushed it right down, leaving it unlatched at the top, and walked quietly back to the hall. On the landing at the head of the stairs Aunt Elizabeth's door was shut. I believe if I had had time I should have gone up and opened it, to see at any price what it was Aunt Elizabeth had in her hands. But I had no time at all. I had not, foolishly, timed myself, but I had taken longer than I had expected.

I went out, shutting the front door softly behind me. I tiptoed round the posts and wire of the playpen, turned up the drive and broke into a run. Before long I was down to a trot on the sharp bend, but once on the level I picked up speed. I ran as I had run the first time between the crowded and silent rhododendrons, but this time the danger was in front of me, not behind. When I reached the top, I stopped for a moment to listen, but I was panting so hard that I could hardly have heard what there might be to hear. I gave it up and ran down to the bridge. Now if the car came I was fairly caught, but there was nothing for it but to go on.

I fell into the driving seat and got the car going in a matter of seconds. I put two hundred yards and a long bend between me and the bridge before I stopped the car and listened again. Somewhere behind and to my left I thought I heard what might be the Morris toiling up the short hill on the far side of the bridge, but the trees muffled the sound and I could not be certain. I drove on sedately towards the point.

The wind got up at sunset, and by the time I was back in the Grane woods you could not have heard an army corps moving with reasonable discretion through the trees fifty yards away. Personal explorers like myself might have converged on the house from all angles and become aware of each other for the first time only outside the back door. I went ahead boldly and met no one. There was the usual cloud-bank, and it was very dark.

I had hoped for darkness indoors as well, but the lights were on in Aunt Elizabeth's sitting-room. I did not know where Coster might be at this hour. The lit windows were solidly curtained. I tried the front door tentatively and found it locked. I went to my window to make sure all was well. My knife blade slid under the bottom of the sash, and a little pressure raised it enough for me to get my finger-tips under it. I raised it gently, put my head inside and listened. There was nothing, but it was no good going in yet. Better the damp woods than the bottled memory of Jock. I went back to the other side of the gravel sweep and prepared to wait.

I did not know when Aunt Elizabeth went to bed. Come to that, I did not know what she did with herself until bed-time. She did not seem to be a Braille reader, and I could not imagine her, even with those incongruously delicate hands, doing knitting or basket work. There was, of course, a wireless in the sitting-room. Not, as far as I remembered, in the bedroom. She might for all I knew sit up until sound broadcasting was over for the night. With the windows shut and curtained and the chaos of the night outside I could not have heard a brass band going full bat upstairs.

The lights went on in the bedroom, in fact, sooner than I had hoped for. For some time they were on in both rooms, and there were lights going on and off in various places that suggested preparations for bed. I imagined Coster took part in these. No blind woman ever took down or put up that elaborate coiffure by herself, and the similarity of style was unmistakable. Ultimately the sitting-room lights went out, leaving those in the bedroom still on. I saw no other lights anywhere, but still did not know where Coster was. I would not have put it past her to sit up cleaning silver or something till all hours. So long as she did not take it into her head to check the dining-room windows I did not mind much what she did.

I waited like this for some time, but the bedroom light stayed on. I suppose if I had thought it would have occurred to me that to Aunt Elizabeth herself lights meant nothing. She might sleep with them on. On the other hand, they might mean a final visit from Coster still due. In fact, I yielded not to reason but to impatience. There was only a limited range of senses deployed against me. So long as the enemy forces were not concentrated, I had to be either invisible or inaudible, but not both. I walked round the western curve of the playpen and opened the dining-room window. Once more I put my head in, listened and heard nothing. I cocked a leg over the sill and climbed in. I wondered about the sash and finally decided to lower it to a point where it looked more or less shut, but I could still open it quickly and silently if I had to.

The dog-heavy air closed round me. I felt committed, almost unbearably excited but not unduly nervous. I let my eyes grow more fully accustomed to the darkness and then began to work my way towards the hall. I wondered for an uncomfortable moment whether Coster locked the dining-room door at night, but when I tried it it gave at once.

I made my way past the passage that led to the kitchens and the bottom of the back stairs. I reached the foot of the main stairs, put my hand on the newel post of the banisters and once more stopped and listened. As I stood there in the dark, with my ears stretched to their utmost sensitivity, someone began knocking loudly on the locked front door.

If I had been a cat, I should have shot straight into the air and come down facing towards the door. Humanly speaking, my reaction was a very creditable attempt. Whether or not my feet actually left the ground, the feeling of convulsive upward movement was very convincing. The knocking went on, not excited or panic-stricken, but very steady and demanding. Bang, bang, bang, it went. Then a pause. Then bang, bang, bang again.

I do not know how often this triple knock had sounded, but I had still not achieved any logical reaction when a door opened upstairs. It was opened in darkness, but there was a glow of indirect light behind it. I stepped back, felt a curtain behind me and scrambled behind it. It was some sort of cupboard or recess, full of hanging clothes. There were coats and macintoshes and what felt like rubber boots under my feet. It smelt musty and horrible. My movement was clumsy, but was masked by a fresh burst of knocking on the front door. Then the lights went on in the hall, but still not at the top of the stairs.

I was peering between curtains at the side of the main staircase. I fancied I was reasonably invisible, but as my only opponent at the moment was Aunt Elizabeth, it presumably did not matter much whether I was or not.

119

Bang, bang, bang, went the knocker, and I suddenly saw
the bottom half of Aunt Elizabeth standing at the top of
the stairs. She called, 'Coster! Coster!' Her voice was tuned
to the peculiar low-pitched resonance which I suppose was
most likely to penetrate the occluded eardrums in another
part of the house. Bang, bang, bang, went the knocker
again, still not very loud, but maddeningly persistent and
demanding. Aunt Elizabeth spoke up in her ordinary voice.
She said, 'Damn the half-wit,' and started to come downstairs. She wore a long red dressing-gown. She was bent
forward, and her yellow-white hair, brushed out quite loose,
hung all round her face.

It was all over in a couple of seconds, but it takes time
to describe. The head, with its mane of swinging hair, suddenly gathered speed, leaving the rest of her behind. The
two small white hands, followed by red sleeves, came
forward clutching at nothing. Then the whole huge red
body launched out in a violent parabola. I had an instan-
taneous, but uncannily detailed, picture of two large feet,
blue-veined round the ankles and wearing a man's check
carpet slippers, neatly disposed side by side as they followed
the red curve of the body. Then she hit the bottom of the
stairs. I did not hear her utter a sound as she fell, but the
muffled thud was tremendous. There were a couple of
smaller, bundling sounds and then dead silence. The knocking had stopped.

I parted the curtains cautiously and looked, not down,
but up at the banisters. On the third post from the top,
about six inches above the tread of the stair, there was a
double turn of plastic-coated wire. The top of the stairs
was still in semi-darkness, and I could not see anything else.
As I turned my eyes down to the bottom of the stairs, Coster
ran out of the passage-way from the kitchens. She was still
fully dressed. I retired behind my curtain and watched her
through the join. She said, 'Ooh—' on a curious long moan-

ing note and plumped herself down by the red wreck of Aunt Elizabeth. I could see very little of either of them, but presently there was a shuffling noise, and one of the check carpet slippers slid out between the banister posts on the second step and flopped down on the floor of the hall. This not being the story of Mr Bedzy, the shoe was empty. Whether Aunt Elizabeth was any less dead for that I did not know. I did not even know whether I wanted her dead or not. The thing hung on a precarious balance of advantage.

Coster went off in one of her intoned running commentaries. I could catch the words only intermittently, but she seemed to be going over Aunt Elizabeth piecemeal, ticking off a sort of mental list as she went. 'Head up now,' I heard. 'Neck's all right. Got a proper old bang, though.' The sound trailed on, and presently I heard her say, 'Ankle looks terrible. Broke, I reckon.'

Then Aunt Elizabeth started to swear. She swore quietly and intermittently, cutting across but not interrupting Coster's monologue. Coster certainly could not hear her, and I doubt if she heard Coster. The effect was breathtaking, but almost impossible to describe. It sounded like someone making fierce noises on a bassoon against the chanter continuo of a bagpipe. 'Wrist swelled right up,' Coster intoned. 'Bloody stair,' Aunt Elizabeth muttered darkly. 'Bloody, bloody, bloody stairs.' 'Sprained,' chanted Coster, 'sprained by the look of it.'

Quite suddenly and distinctly Aunt Elizabeth said, 'Damn,' and the chanting stopped. In the sudden silence something—I do not know whether it was the faintest sound or a movement in the corner of my eye—brought my attention back to the banisters above me. I was just in time to see a flicker of movement, like the tail of a vanishing snake. The wire had gone. Somebody up in the shadow had cast off a standing end on the far side of the stair and pulled the wire in.

121

I could not do anything. Coster, muttering softly again over Aunt Elizabeth, blocked my way to the bottom of both staircases, whereas whoever it was up there had the back stairs and the two back doors at their disposal. Whether they had seen me among the hanging macintoshes I did not know, but I doubted it.

Aunt Elizabeth had stopped swearing, but moaned slightly at intervals. Coster's muttering was only spasmodic, and there was something of a struggle going on at the foot of the stairs. Then a moan turned to a grunt as the air was squeezed out behind it. There was a fierce catch of breath, and Aunt Elizabeth's red dressing-gown heaved suddenly into view, bent at an acute angle. Incredibly, but there before my eyes, Coster stood on the second stair up with Aunt Elizabeth flung over her shoulder. To say, as Claudia had said, that she was as strong as an ox was evidently a wild understatement. She ought to have been in a circus. Step by step, with one hand on the banisters and the other steadying her load, she made her way upstairs. Aunt Elizabeth's head hung down behind the square black shoulders. I could not see the face, but the neck was livid and the long mane of ivory-coloured hair rustled against the hem of Coster's skirt. I thought if the fall had not killed her this would, coming on top of it.

They reached the top of the stairs, and Coster went steadily along the passage and through the door of the sitting-room. I stepped out into the hall and listened. Upstairs there was a prodigious creak of springs as the huge inert body was dumped on the bed. Then the telephone bell on the wall above me pinged faintly, and I knew Coster had lifted the receiver. It was time I went.

I still could not risk going up the main stairs, not with the door of Aunt Elizabeth's room standing wide open. I considered the back stairs, but was put off by the thought of walking up them in the dark, when there might still be someone at the top with a length of plastic-covered wire in their hands.

I could hear Coster talking in a normal voice into the telephone. I walked through the hall, turned into the dark dining-room and went to my window. Very cautiously I opened it and put my head out. The night was still pitch-black and noisy. I climbed out and shut the window down behind me.

The walk back to the car was not the most enjoyable part of my evening. The woods threshed and roared round me, and I kept wondering where, in this roaring darkness, was the person with the wire. Whoever they were, they were too ingenious by half.

I told Henry I had been to the pictures in Swincombe and had not thought much of them. He nodded sympathetically and said there was not much going on round here. I did not argue the point.

14

By what I must regard, in the absence of any evidence to
the contrary, as pure chance, I saw Claudia quite early next
day. The Morris was parked outside a chemist's in the
square, and she came out with half-a-dozen small parcels.
She said, 'Hullo, Johnnie. Aunt Elizabeth's had an accident.'

'Oh? Fatal, I hope?'

'Not yet, anyway. She fell downstairs. Coster found her
at the bottom. This was late last night. No one knows what
she was doing on the stairs at the time. Coster thought she
heard something, and came out and found her.'

'What does she say herself?'

'Aunt Elizabeth? She doesn't say anything. She's fairly
heavily concussed and pretty dopey. The doctor says she
very likely won't remember much what happened anyway.'

'But she'll survive?'

'She'll survive all right. She's got a badly twisted ankle
and probably a broken wrist, and she's bruised all over and,
as I say, concussed, but it will take more than that to kill
my Aunt Elizabeth.'

'It could have been her neck. She must weigh all of fourteen or fifteen stone.'

'Well, it wasn't.'

I clucked my sympathy. 'And now you're nursing her?'

'Not me. Coster. I do the shopping.'

'Oughtn't she to be in hospital?'

'She's not, anyhow. She's flat on her back on her own
bed, snoring slightly, with Coster in attendance.'

My heart sank. I said, 'Is Coster with her all night?'

Claudia hesitated for a moment, looking at me. Then she said, 'There wasn't any night last night. It was all coming and going. Tonight—yes, I suppose Coster will bed down near her.'

I nodded. I was tormented by the thought of Aunt Elizabeth knocked out in her bedroom and Coster, with the strength of a professional weight lifter, asleep in the sitting-room. What I said was, 'Well, that lets you out at least. Can't we meet? It's been an awful long time.'

'Not tonight, Johnnie, I don't think. I shall have to dance attendance for a bit, in case she comes round and finds I'm not there.'

'But you're not going out to live in that place?'

'Not that, no. But I'd better be on call. And I must go now. But some time, Johnnie, yes?'

'Some time soon,' I said. She got herself and her parcels into the car and went off towards Grane.

I think if I had seen the car while she was still inside the shop I should have opened the boot and had a look inside. It is just the sort of place one throws a non-committal thing like a length of plastic-coated wire when one has stopped using it. Come to that, half the car boots in the country may contain lengths of plastic-coated wire, though the owners cannot all have rich aunts who fall downstairs in the night. Anyway, I had not looked.

But I was obsessed with the feeling that time was running out. Someone had got rid of the dog and now someone, whether the same person or not, had made a very convincing attempt at getting rid of Aunt Elizabeth. The only person, as far as I knew, who specifically needed Aunt Elizabeth dead was Claudia. There might, of course, be others. What Claudia had told me about her aunt's dispositions might be mistaken, or at least incomplete. It might also have been deliberately false, but I did not at that stage see why it should be.

If Claudia was the nocturnal wire-puller, I did not grudge her an ultimate success. With a large part of my mind I really wanted her free of her burden and enjoying the family money. I grudged her, indeed, nothing but the one piece of her aunt's property I wanted myself. If it had not been Claudia, I found the implications much harder to bear. If the person who was so busy about putting Aunt Elizabeth out of the way did not merely want her dead, I did not like to think what he might want.

Worry and speculation apart, one fact nagged at me ceaselessly. Whereas last night I had been up against one pair of eyes and one pair of ears, tonight only the eyes would be left. Aunt Elizabeth, out to the wide, would be in her bedroom. Coster, as formidable, once roused, as a devoted gorilla, but as deaf as a post, would be in attendance. If only she was in the bedroom with Aunt Elizabeth, I could use gelignite on the wall-cupboard and still work undisturbed. I had not, of course, got any gelignite, but I did not think it would be necessary. Nor, considering what I expected the cupboard to contain, really advisable. I drove into Swincombe and bought myself a heavy screwdriver and one of those formidable instruments for opening packing cases and levering out nails that are as near a jemmy as an honest man should ever be found in possession of. I waited for the night, and wished Aunt Elizabeth a deeper unconsciousness.

When the night at last came, it came pitch dark and dead quiet. As the only member of the party with an active sense of hearing, I found this very welcome. With the woods threshing and moaning round the house I was not much better off than Coster. In this sort of drugged silence, I could hear her skirts swishing at fifty yards, even if she was not thinking aloud. In fact, all I hoped to have to listen for was movement in the next room. Once get Coster located and immobile on the other side of the connecting doorway, and I reckoned I could always get from the wall-cupboard on to the landing before she got the door open. The one thing I feared was that she should decide to bed down in the sitting-room. I pictured her lying rigid on some sort of truckle-bed with her huge chest going up and down in sleep. I did not know at all what I might do then. But the chances were that she would not risk a door between her and her charge—if, indeed, she slept at all. She did not look as if she needed to.

I left the car up a side turning, and well hidden at that. I walked all of two miles to the bridge. I had a webbing strap round my waist and from this the jemmy on one side and the screwdriver on the other hung down the outside of my leg inside the trouser. They did not hinder my walking as much as I had anticipated. Not even the jemmy was long enough to reach below the bend of my knee. I had a torch in my pocket but nothing else except my knife, which was my constant and legitimate companion.

I tiptoed over the bridge. It was so dark that I could barely see the gleam of water in the creek. I had rather lost track of the tides, but the creek seemed fairly full. The air was clear, but wringing wet and almost rancid with the smell of leaf mould and rotting wood. I have never heard such abject silence.

I tiptoed the whole way down that cavernous drive. It did not seem safe to do anything else. Coster was safe enough, but there was still the unknown with the clever ideas and the plastic-coated wire. Whoever they were, they knew their way around and might be anywhere.

Before the drive turned down to the carriage-sweep I turned out into the bushes and looked over the back of the house. There were no lights anywhere. Whether or not Coster was on duty in the sick-room, she was not in the kitchens. The front of the house, when I came to it, showed what I had expected and what was, on the whole, the most

I could hope for. There was a light—but faint, even behind the curtains—in the bedroom and none anywhere else. Down here, between the face of the house and the semi-circular wall of trees, the monstrous silence felt thick enough to touch. It took me five minutes to walk across the gravel; and when I came to the window I found it latched.

For the first time—really for the first time, despite the excitement and the nervous tension of it—a faint sense of unease crept into me. Someone, since Aunt Elizabeth had plunged downstairs the night before, had done the rounds, found a window unlatched and latched it. I did not think I had left any signs of disturbance on the window. Fingerprints, no doubt, by the dozen, but it was not Scotland Yard I was up against. All the same, someone had found a gap in the defences and closed it. What they had thought when they found it I did not know. If, as seemed overwhelmingly probable, it had been Coster, she had probably not thought anything. Only I had rather it had not been found at all. And I had certainly very much rather the window had not been re-latched. Once I had loosened it up from inside I could probably, in fact, get it open again with my knife blade. I did not want to have to try. I left it and tiptoed off round the end of the house. There was no car anywhere. The garage door was shut, but I shone a torch briefly through a side window on to empty concrete. Claudia might be standing by, but she was not, apparently, at the bedside. I made my way, still with the same infinite caution, round to the back. It was just possible, I thought, that if Coster was still in circulation she had not locked both back doors or latched all the back windows. I did not favour climbing in across the kitchen sink, but better that than try to force the dining-room window.

The first door, which I thought led direct into the kitchen, was certainly locked. The second was the door I had stumbled out of over the spreadeagled body of Jock. I did

128

not like, even now, to think of the dark floor space inside between the whitewashed walls. I remembered there was an old-fashioned drop latch on this door, and they can be noisy things. When I came to it, I raised the latch very carefully. The door opened at once under my hand and the pitch darkness inside was waiting for me to step into it.

I wrestled with an almost overpowering temptation to flash my torch on to the floor before I stepped on it, but this was plainly nonsense. In the circumstances it would not matter much if I knocked a table over, but to start flashing lights about might be fatal. It was not, of course, a table I was really worrying about. I stepped in and shut the door behind me. The flagstones were reassuringly hard under my feet, and I felt better.

I stood there, hoping that if I waited long enough I might be able to see something. In fact, the darkness outside had been so intense that there was not much more my eyes could do. I thought I saw, over to my right, the outline of the door I knew was there. It led into the stone-flagged passage which went past Jock's lair and ultimately into the hall. Before it got there it passed the foot of the back stairs. It was these I intended to use. Whether or not it was any safer, it seemed more respectful.

I made my way to the door and found it standing open. Despite the proximity of Jock's lair, the smell of him was less here than it had been in the front of the house. I fancied the stone flags, no doubt ruthlessly scrubbed, held the offence less ineradicably than the boards and carpets above stairs. I went very slowly along the passage, one hand on the wall and one out in front of me. I put down each foot as a separate and calculated operation. Presently the wall on my left ended, and I smelt rather than saw the upward cavern of the back staircase. Then someone began marching upstairs.

It was certainly Coster. The weight might have been Aunt

Elizabeth's but even if she was up and about, which seemed impossible, Aunt Elizabeth's walk was quite different. Only Coster marched. She marched to a door and opened it. There was a click and the upstairs lights went on. Then she was on the march again.

For a moment of agonised concentration I tried to hear which stairs she was coming down. That she was coming down I never for some reason doubted. The heavy footsteps went right along the landing. As they passed the top of the front stairs I started to run. She had not put the hall lights on, but there was a reflected glow from upstairs which was like daylight after what I had been through. She paused, clicked on another switch and started down the back stairs. She even marched downstairs. Step by step with her, although sound was of no importance, I marched up the front.

I stood on the landing, half-way between the two stair-heads, and waited to see what she would do. Aunt Elizabeth's sitting-room was in darkness, but the door through to the bedroom was half open. There was a light inside, but not a bright one. Coster was doing things downstairs in the kitchen. I heard taps turned on and the sound of crockery. She had started to drone over her occupation, but it was impossible at this distance to tell what she was saying. Whatever she was doing, it seemed to take a very long time. The only person who was upstairs with me was blind and semi-conscious, but I still did not like standing there on the lit landing.

There was nothing else I could do. Sooner or later Coster would come marching up one or the other of the staircases, and when she did the only safe thing was for me to march down the other. I had to stay between them, and when Coster had left the landing light turned on it was certainly not for me to turn it off. I stood there, with one hand on the landing railing, wishing that she would get

130

through her little errand of mercy and hurry back to the sick-room.

I had just begun to lose my concentration when I heard her feet on the stone flags of the passage. She must have carried quite a bit of metal on her shoes. She clanked like a guardsman in a palace yard. She was past the foot of the back stairs before I realised it, and it was touch and go. Luckily, she paused to switch on the hall lights, and by the time she reached the bottom of the main staircase, I was on the top stair of the back.

I went down as she went up. It was like an old-fashioned barometer, only vertical instead of horizontal. There seemed to be lights everywhere now. Too many lights, only I could not turn them out. She began to go along the landing, hesitated, stopped and turned back. For a moment I almost believed she was coming down the back stairs again, and was gathering myself for another dash to the main stairs when she stopped. It was the lights. She clicked two switches on the landing, and the lights went out in the hall and on the main staircase. Then she resumed her march, paused at the door of the sitting-room and clicked out the landing lights. Everything was in darkness now except the back stairs, where I lingered coyly on the bottom step, casting a long embarrassing shadow across the flagstones of the passage. I was wondering whether I could possibly put the staircase light out when Coster noticed her mistake.

She said, quite audibly, 'Oh dear, now, the backstairs light.' She put whatever she was carrying down with a clink and marched back along the landing. I retreated to the darkness of the scullery until the light was out on the stairs, and I heard her tramp back along the landing, pick up her baggage, go into the sitting-room and shut the door after her. Everything was dark again. We were back to square one.

This time I chose the back stairs. Even if they did seem

to be Coster's favourite way down, they did at least screen me from the sitting-room door until I emerged on to the landing. I went up them with infinite caution, despite the two shut doors between me and Coster's vestigial sense of hearing. The landing was dark as pitch and absolutely silent. I tiptoed to the sitting-room door and opened it. The room was in darkness, but there was a faint glow of light from under the bedroom door. Nothing moved in the bedroom and no one spoke. However Coster had decided to spent the night, my guess was that she had started spending it.

After the darkness outside, the faint glow under the door seemed surprisingly adequate lighting. I found my way without mishap to the wall-cupboard. Then I looked towards the landing door. There was a chair blocking my line of retreat. I went back and moved it. The door stood open. I turned to the cupboard.

It was solid woodwork with some sort of mortice lock and a very small keyhole. It did not look formidable. I put my hand to my waistband and started to pull the jemmy up out of my trouser leg.

Claudia said, 'Didn't Mr Levinson tell you where it was kept, Johnnie?' She must have had one of those enormous torches with a handle and a pound's worth of dry battery in it. I was floodlit as ruthlessly as Somerset House.

I said, 'Hullo, Claudia. No, should he have?' I felt completely hollow, but was conscious that the vacuum was filling slowly with a black seething rage. She came into the room and shut the landing door behind her.

She said, 'We can't talk here. Come on outside, will you? We don't want to rouse the house.'

There was a moment's silence. Then I said, 'There's someone walking downstairs.' I made for the door. She stood with her back to it, still shining her monstrous light in my face. 'Johnnie, Johnnie,' she said, 'don't go away. We must talk.' She did not move.

'Of course I'll talk,' I said. 'But first let me get out.' I reached out suddenly and put the torch aside. A moment later I had her by the shoulders. All I did was put her aside. I opened the door, switched on my own torch and ran down the stairs. I followed the passage to the scullery and could smell, even before I got there, the back door I had used standing wide open to the night outside.

As I came back to the bottom of the stairs, Claudia shut the door of the sitting-room and started along the landing. I stood and waited for her. 'I'm at your disposal,' I said.

15

We walked slowly up the drive side by side. It was still
pitch dark. The rage had died out of me and I felt empty
again. I had no resentment against Claudia at all. I put out
a hand and touched her on the shoulder. 'I am like your
Aunt Elizabeth,' I said. 'I dislike walking alone when there
are people about.'

She winced under my hand and I said, 'What's the
trouble? Aunt Elizabeth?'

'You don't know?'

'No. Why should I?'

'Never mind, Johnnie.' She put a hand on my arm, and
we walked like that, close but not touching except for her
hand through my sleeve. We went to her car, which she
had left out along the road to the point. I had only once
before been in it. It was very much a personal possession
and smelt very strongly of her. I do not think anyone else
ever went in it much, except for her ferrying of Coster.
Coster, whatever her faults, smelt of nothing. She turned
it and we drove back towards Dunstreet. She drove very
slowly. I do not know what time it was.

After a bit she said, 'You've never seen the saucer?'

'The saucer?'

'The tazza. It's always been called the Queen's Saucer in
this family. You've never seen it, of course—only the photographs.'

'No. How should I have?'

'It's been in the family a long time without causing any
particular excitement. There is some legendary connection
with Queen Elizabeth. I forget the details. The eldest

134

daughter seems always to be called Elizabeth.'

'She probably slept here.'

'It's more solid than that. She gave an early Barton a monopoly or something. Anyway, she made the family, in the way it could happen then. She is supposed to have given him the saucer. I suppose it's likely enough. It must have belonged to her, after all, unless Giacomo never got his presentation set accepted.'

'Set? You haven't got a dozen of these things?'

'We haven't, no. But I've always assumed he presented the Queen with something like a set of glass. He would have, wouldn't he? She gave this Barton one as a souvenir, and it has been kept safe as a family trophy. The others I imagine were used in the royal household until they were dropped, one by one, by the royal servants. Our saucer was treated as a relic from the start, and only that survived. It's got a special box that must be a couple of hundred years old itself.'

I said, 'We'd better not leave my car outside all night. It's up the side road on the left here.'

'I'll take you to it.'

'But Claudia, I've got to know about this. Can I come to Lower West Street?'

She stopped the Morris where I told her, and suddenly leant her head on her hands, which still held the wheel. She spoke without lifting it or looking at me. 'All right, Johnnie. Come along now. I'll be expecting you.'

The first thing I noticed was that the Interesting Ale was no longer in position on the mantelpiece. I said, 'You haven't smashed it?'

'The ale? No, no. It's put away safe. I also have my family relic.'

'I'll have a special box made. Now go on about the tazza.'

'As I said, it's never caused much excitement. Lots of

135

families have their relics. But Aunt Elizabeth's got a thing
about it. I don't know what it is, and I shouldn't care to
ask her. I think it's something to do with her being Elizabeth and the last of the Bartons. Anyway, she adores it,
and it has got worse with her blindness. She won't let it out
of her hands, literally. No one else is allowed to touch it.'

'Does she know its value?'

'I don't think the idea of a cash value ever occurred to
her. That was me. I saw the sale of the K.Y. Goblet reported
and did a bit of homework on Giacomo Verzelini. What is
it worth, Johnnie?'

'I don't know. No one knows. I don't like to think of it.'

'Then why try to steal it?'

I looked at her. I do not know what expression I had on
my face, but she suddenly threw back her head and laughed
that terrible ringing laugh I had heard once before. She
said, 'God help you, Johnnie, I believe you love it for itself
alone.' We sat back in our corners of the sofa, looking at
each other with hopeless misunderstanding. Her whole
face had changed again. I nodded. 'Of course,' I said. 'I
couldn't sell a thing like that. There's nothing very noble
about it.'

'No? No, I suppose not. You're mad, of course, but on
the whole I'd rather it was that way. Old Mr Levinson was
the same.'

'Tell me about him. How did it happen?'

'That was my doing. I told you—I did my homework
and got the idea that if the thing was what it claimed to be
it was pretty fabulous. I thought if there was anything here
worth that sort of money I'd like to know about it, at least.
I don't think I'd gone any further in my mind at that stage.
And of course, I didn't want Aunt Elizabeth to know. It
took a bit of organising.'

'What did you do?'

'I wrote to Levinson. His books are in the County Library

136

and he seemed pretty eminent. I hoped he was respectable. Well, so he was, only— Anyway, I wrote to him asking him whether I could consult him in complete confidence about a piece of glass I believed to be of considerable interest. I had a reassuring letter back, and I then sent him an account of the saucer with its inscription. He wrote back in a kind of tremendous scholarly excitement, saying he would be greatly in my debt if I could arrange for him to see it and, if possible, photograph it. I asked him to come and see me at Dunstreet and discuss the matter, and he came.

'I gave him a fairly honest account of the position. I said my old blind aunt treasured the thing to the point of queerness and would never agree to its leaving her possession or even being examined. If he didn't mind a little mild deception I could arrange for him to be in the room unknown to her while she had it out, and he might even be able to photograph it in her hands, but that was the best I could do. If he wanted to see it like this he must promise me not to make his presence known.

'He was doubtful—he was rather a grand old man, wasn't he?—but his passion to know was too much for his scruples. He agreed, and I brought him along. I put him in a corner of the room, unknown to Aunt Elizabeth, and got her to show me the saucer. That was easy if you knew the approach. She turned it over and over and round and round in her hands, as she always does—you've never seen her with it—and when old Levinson started firing off his flashes I made covering up noises. Aunt Elizabeth did once ask me why I was so restless, but I don't think she suspected anything.

'I got Levinson away and we came back here. He was frantic with excitement, poor old thing. He said he must publish the discovery. I said my aunt's name and the whereabouts of the saucer must not be mentioned in any circumstances. I said there was no way of protecting the thing, as it is here, from the attentions of undesirable characters once its whereabouts and value were known. There isn't really, is there, Johnnie?'

'You're not doing badly,' I said.

'And of course, more to the point, Aunt Elizabeth would never forgive me for what I had done. It would finish me altogether if the thing came out. He said would I allow him to publish a report with photos if he promised me solemnly not to reveal its whereabouts or ownership to anyone? He pointed out that the more publicity it had now, the higher price it would eventually command. He seemed to think that argument would appeal to me.'

'Funny,' I said. 'Anyway, you agreed.'

'Yes. I agreed to his publishing a report on the saucer in a learned journal, with unidentifiable photographs, on the condition that everything else was kept secret. He promised this solemnly. He published. And then he died. And somehow something went wrong, didn't it, Johnnie? Someone got to know more than they were supposed to.'

'Only me,' I said. 'At least—only me, so far as I know.'

'How?'

'I don't think that matters. Pure chance. And I've certainly told nobody.'

'What did Mr Levinson tell you?'

'Nothing. At the time of his death I knew only what was in the published report.'

'You didn't find it necessary to remove him, did you, Johnnie? I hope not. I liked old Mr Levinson.'

'Not me. Nor anyone else. I found him dead, but he had died of a heart attack. Didn't you see the inquest report?'

'No. But you found him? You were on the spot pretty quick, weren't you, Johnnie?'

'I went there by appointment with Mr Levinson. It wasn't my fault if he was dead when I got there.'

'And found Aunt Elizabeth's name and address on a

138

paper in his pocket? No, on second thoughts, knowing you, it couldn't have been in his pocket. On his desk, say?'

I said, 'No, you gave me those.'

'But you found enough to bring you down here?'

'I found enough to bring me down here, yes. Just that. And then I met a beautiful girl at a glass auction, and she fed me on lobster in Elfhame, and one thing sort of led to another.'

'But nothing led to the saucer, Johnnie.'

'One thing did finally, and that, I must admit, I had, directly or indirectly, from Levinson. But you showed me where to look for it.'

'And now you've lost it. You know that, don't you?' We sat there looking at each other from our opposite ends of the sofa. I think for the moment my detachment was almost as blank as hers. Finally, I said, 'I suppose so, yes. So long as nobody else gets it.'

'There is nobody else. Why should there be? The thing must remain in Aunt Elizabeth's hands till she dies. That is essential, Johnnie—for me, I mean. You must understand that. If the thing were taken from her now, I don't know what she might do, but I know I'd suffer for it. Whether you care to consider her feelings is up to you.'

'I'm not ready to be over-sensitive about them, I don't think. You don't think the shock would kill her?'

'I don't for a moment. She might be driven nearly round the bend with a sense of outrage and baffled fury, and, as I say, I don't know what she might not do. But she'd survive. It wouldn't be nice, though. Not for any of us.'

'All right. Supposing she dies with the thing still in her possession? Then it would be yours?'

'Then it would be mine, yes.'

'And what would you do with it? Sell it, wouldn't you?'

She looked at me as if I somehow shared the remoteness of her speculation. Even at that distance she spoke very

139

directly to me. She said, 'That would depend on how she died, and when. Let me put it like this. We don't know what the saucer is worth, to me, in cash. But it is no more than a part of Aunt Elizabeth's assets. Even on a cash basis her death would be worth much more to me than the value of the saucer. And there are not only cash considerations involved. But I can do nothing until she is dead.'

We went on looking at each other. Then I said, 'I will certainly let you put it like that. No one, indeed, could put it better. Let me for my part consider the position you so clearly state and see what, if anything, can be done about it. There's one more thing. Is there anyone here who knows, or could have found out, enough about your saucer to connect it with Levinson's report, if he happened to see it? You say the thing has caused no great excitement for years past. Equally, I suppose, it has not been kept a jealously guarded secret. There may be people who know of its existence and origin. Are there, in fact?'

She shook her head. 'Only Seaton.'

'That's the solicitor. You've mentioned him before. You said he was all right.'

'So he is. He knows the thing exists, and I thought it wise to tell him about Levinson's visit and report. But he won't say anything. I've seen to that.'

I thought, again, that I should like to see this Seaton. Claudia seemed to have him fully under control. I wondered whether it amounted to professional misconduct in a solicitor to be seduced by his client. Probably that was only doctors. But I might be wrong. Seaton might be a venerable and respectable father-figure. Even so—I jerked my mind away from the unknown Seaton and said, 'No one else at all?'

'No one. Why? Are you still being followed?'

'I've told you. Like Aunt Elizabeth, I feel there are people about.'

'And you don't like that?' She smiled at me. The smile had a slightly maternal, indulgent quality which in Claudia was completely exasperating, and yet so attractive that my whole mind melted as I sat and looked at it. She said, 'Never mind, Johnnie. I'll look after things. Are you going back to London?'

I longed to say I was not, but I so obviously was that it was not worth arguing. I merely nodded. Claudia said, 'I'll miss you, you know.' And I did know. Despite everything else I knew, I knew Claudia would in fact miss me. As for me, I knew only too well what I was letting myself in for.

I moved towards her, and was brought up short by the jemmy in my trouser leg. She sat back at her end of the sofa, looking at me with her head a little on one side. Three times, so far as I remembered, I had seen her like that before, but the picture was now a built-in part of my mind. I got up and for the second time that night began to drag the ironmongery up out of my waistband.

Even Claudia looked a little startled. She said, 'What's this, Johnnie? Something new? I don't think—'

I said, 'Don't worry. Unarm, Eros. The long day's task is done.' I pulled the screwdriver out of the other trouser leg and laid it beside the jemmy on the seat of an early Victorian armchair. It must have rejected them, because as I turned back to Claudia they slipped to the ground with a tremendous metallic clatter. I left them there.

Claudia began laughing again, and this time I joined her. We laughed so much I could hardly come to grips with her. She put her head back and said, 'It wasn't in the cupboard, you know, Johnnie. It wasn't in the cupboard at all. And you all tooled up—' She pointed helplessly to the hardware on the carpet and began to shake with laughter again. I took her by the shoulders and she winced, as she had done in the drive, but this time I held her firmly and fairly shook the laughter out of her.

I walked about Dunstreet in what must have been the small hours of the morning. I had lost all count of time and was not sufficiently curious to look at my watch. The thing seemed to be at an end, but nothing was settled. It seemed equally impossible to leave Claudia or stay with her. I could not get the tazza out of my head, but could not bend my mind to the serious and reasonable calculation of the only course which, as I very well knew, could now bring me to it.

In any case I had to get to London. There was something I wanted to know, and might or might not find out there, but could certainly not find out anywhere else. There were lights burning all night in the square at Dunstreet, but the smaller streets were in darkness. I walked about alone in the damp soft air, hardly able to remember the glare and second-hand staleness of London. It was very much as if I had always been there.

Towards morning the air began to move at last, and a stealthy breeze crept in from the direction of the sea, rustling the dead leaves that hung about here and there on the pavements and in the gutters. I was tired out and began to make my way back towards the *Fleur-de-Lys*. Just as I got there, I remembered the name I had been trying to think of. Joachim. That was it, Miss Joachim. Old Levinson may have been a Jew, after all. I wondered where I could find Miss Joachim now. But that could wait till morning.

I tucked the jemmy and screwdriver inside my jacket. Claudia had not wished to add them to her relics and would not have them left on her carpet. It occurred to me now for the first time to consider what even a Dunstreet policeman might have said if he had found me wandering the streets in the small hours with these things sticking out of my pocket. But the man who let me in was too sleepy to notice anything, and I got them upstairs undetected.

16

The house in St John's Wood was still empty. There was a
For Sale notice outside. It was a dramatically desirable
property, and for it to be in the market even this long meant
that old Levinson's family had put a breath-taking price on
it and could afford to sit and wait for a buyer. The agents
were Carmichaels, who are not the sort of people to be
interested in sporting offers. It was going to be a long
business.

Carmichaels were so shocked that anyone should
approach them for any other purpose than buying a house
that it took them some time to formulate a policy and
decide on a course of action. By this time I was two floors
up and on one-inch pile. I explained what I wanted for the
third time. 'I apologise for troubling you,' I said, 'and of
course I know it is no concern of yours. But I hoped you
might be able to help me. I was a friend of Mr Levinson's.
In point of fact, I had the unfortunate experience of finding him dead. But I don't know his family at all, and I
suppose they are the present vendors. I wanted to get in
touch with a previous member of his staff. I feel sure Mr
Levinson's solicitors would know their whereabouts, but I
don't know who they are—the solicitors, I mean. If you
could possibly help me to that extent—'

The executive behind the desk experienced a sudden
revelation. His face became ecstatic. 'You want to know
who are acting for Mr Levinson's estate?' he said.

'I suppose so, yes.'

'You feel they would be able to give you the information
you want?'

143

I said, 'I want to get in touch with the late Mr Levinson's housekeeper, a Miss Joachim. I don't know where she is now, but I feel sure Mr Levinson's solicitors must have an address. If you could tell me who they are, I could ask them, perhaps.' I tried not to make the proposal sound too outrageous.

The man beamed with pleasure. He said, 'Just so, just so,' and breathed heavily through his nose, still beaming. Then he said, 'Well, Mr Slade, I see no reason why we should not help you in this matter. I suggest you see a firm called Russ & Jerrold in Lincoln's Inn Fields. I think you'll find they're the people you want.'

'That's fine,' I said. 'I'll do that.'

I thanked him and made for the door. Before I reached it he was on the phone. I thought my enquiry from Russ & Jerrold would not be unexpected, and it was not. Whether or not there were any Russes or Jerrolds about, the man I saw was called Moss. He was dark where he was not bald and very young and friendly, but was not admitting to any previous knowledge of me.

I went through it all again, and he said, 'I see, yes,' as if the thing seemed fairly intelligible at a first hearing. Then he said, 'And you thought we might be in touch with Miss Joachim?'

'I thought you probably would be, yes.'

He looked more friendly than ever. 'Actually,' he said, 'Miss Joachim is one of the beneficiaries under Mr Levinson's will.'

'Yes. Well, I didn't know, of course, but I thought very likely Mr Levinson would be a man who would make provision for his staff on his death.'

'Yes? Oh yes. Yes, certainly. Well—'

'Look,' I said, 'if I promise not to sell Miss Joachim any gold shares, do you think you could tell me where I can find her?'

This appealed to him tremendously. He said, 'Gold shares, eh? No, indeed. Certainly not. No, well—'

This time I refused to help him out. I just sat and looked at him. Every time he smiled at me, I smiled back with added warmth. The whole room glowed with it. Finally he said, 'Yes, well—' I waited breathlessly. The whole thing might be completely useless, but I was getting my money's worth. 'Actually,' he said, 'I have been handling that matter myself, and I have the address here, I think.' It seemed kinder not to look at him, still less smile. He rooted about among some papers in a top drawer. I got out my diary and pencil. 'Ah, here we are,' he said. 'Miss Joachim is living at 23 Harland Road, Kenton. Not too far, I think.'

'No, indeed. Thank you very much. I'll get in touch with her.' I got up. The door was almost immediately behind me, and he did not have as long to wait as the man at Carmichaels. Even so, his hand was moving towards the telephone as the door shut on our interlocking smiles.

Miss Joachim, by contrast, opened the door to me herself, and said, 'Come in, Mr Slade. I saw you at the inquest, of course, but not since. Mr Marling said you had spoken to him. Did you find your books?'

I said, 'Mr Marling?' I groped desperately in my mind.

'Mr Levinson's chauffeur.'

'Oh yes, of course. I didn't know his name. Yes, thank you. I had left them somewhere else, of course. It was silly of me, but I was a bit upset, you know. If I'd known he'd mentioned it, I'd have rung up, at least, to let you know it was all right. I really am sorry. I hope you didn't waste time looking for them.'

'No, no. I thought perhaps you'd left them somewhere else. Now, what can I do for you, Mr Slade? I am told you do not want to sell me anything.'

She had very smooth grey hair pulled back tight over an ivory forehead. Forty years ago she must have been a

145

proper little Rose of Sharon. She was still full of wicked intelligence. I went straight at it.

'Mr Levinson asked me to call on him at half past ten that night. He said he would be free by then, but had a guest for dinner. I came at half past ten. I never saw anyone else there, and, as you know, I found Mr Levinson very recently dead. I never heard anything more of the dinner guest. Do you know who it was?'

'You realise I have been asked this before?'

'I didn't, no. By whom?'

'By the police, naturally. They wanted to fix the time of Mr Levinson's death as closely as possible. We know he was dead when you got there. They naturally wanted to make sure that he was still alive when his dinner guest left, and, if so, when that was.'

'And did they?'

'No. Because we never knew who it was. And of course when they found that Mr Levinson's death was perfectly natural, and in fact expected, they didn't bother. But—well, that answers your question, doesn't it, Mr Slade?'

'This was all perfectly normal procedure, was it?'

'Oh yes, perfectly normal. Sometimes, of course, Mr Levinson would say who was coming—he didn't entertain much, you know—and sometimes some of the staff had to stay and help, but if there was only one guest—and that would probably be a man—he usually preferred to have dinner left ready and look after his guest himself. If it's any comfort to you, I had no idea you were expected that evening, either. I suppose the appointment was made by telephone?'

'That's right. Earlier the same day.'

'Yes. Well, I can't say when the dinner appointment was made. But probably only the day before, because Mr Levinson only ordered dinner that morning.'

'And there was nothing to show at all who it was?'

Miss Joachim looked at me. We were sitting facing each other in an extraordinary non-committal parlour, which I felt sure could not permanently represent Miss Joachim's tastes or interests. She said, 'I don't know, Mr Slade. Perhaps you wouldn't mind telling me. This is nothing to do with Mr Levinson's death, is it?'

'Nothing whatever. No, it's about the business I came to see him about. I'm interested in antique glass myself, though nothing like on Mr Levinson's scale. But I—I have since had reason to wonder whether he had already discussed it with someone else. As I never found him alive, you see, I could not hear this from him. If it comes to that, I suppose I thought of the dinner guest because I knew there was one. But anyone he saw during the last day or two before his death—anyone interested in glass, I mean. I suppose you don't know of anyone?'

'I'm afraid not. There is one thing. Very shortly before he died Mr Levinson did say something about someone he was expecting to see. He would never discuss particular people, naturally—not with me, I mean—but he did sometimes make a general remark which reflected obliquely on someone he'd seen or something he'd been dealing with, or was going to deal with. I knew him very well, you know. I'd been with him a great many years. I can't remember exactly when this was, but I know it was only just before he died. He said—you'll have to excuse this, Mr Slade—not that it's very offensive. Mr Levinson was a Jew, of course, as I am myself, and sometimes, naturally, we talk about you —about people who are not Jews—in general terms, just as you, I've no doubt, talk about Jews. He said something jokingly about God's promise to Moses that his people should lend to other people and not borrow, and said—I forget his exact words—that other people always expected us to put up the money—something like that. Anyhow, I know I got the impression that he was talking about some

147

proposition that was going to be put to him and that he did not intend to accept. But it's all very vague. Of course, I don't know what your business with him was, Mr Slade.'

I smiled at her. 'Not money, Miss Joachim. Glass. And it was only his expert opinion I wanted on that. So if he was expecting someone to try to touch him, it wasn't me. I suppose it might have been the dinner guest. Whoever it was, I imagine he stood firm on the intention he implied to you. I mean—he is not known to have made any sort of advance to anyone just before his death?'

'I don't think so. I should not necessarily know, perhaps. But I have no doubt, from the way he spoke, that in this particular case he did not intend to. In any case, if your business with him was only glass, this can be of no concern to you.' Miss Joachim's pleasant voice sharpened suddenly to an edge and broke off short. I got up.

'No,' I said. 'Well, it can't be helped. I'm very grateful to you and I'm sorry I've taken up your time. At least I haven't tried to sell you anything.'

Miss Joachim shook her head that little bit more than an English woman would have shaken it. She smiled and was all warmth again. 'No? No, well perhaps that is just as well. I think you would have a very good selling line, Mr Slade. And we unprotected women—you know what it is.' We parted with much mutual approval. I wondered what, if anything, I had gained.

I got back into London at that uncomfortable hour of the afternoon when the people in the offices are working against the clock to get through the things they would have done earlier if they had not taken so long over lunch. No one has started going home yet, or even drinking, but the terrible mass frustration of the office worker is working itself quietly up to boiling point. I always go to a good tea shop, preferably one where the tables are in separate alcoves. There are a few left in a wilderness of espressos. An old innocence lingers in them. Tea must now be the only drink that carries no taint of licence. I suppose that is because the young no longer drink it. I sipped a mild commercial Keemun and tried to think consecutively.

All I got was a chaos of alternating incompatibles. My better nature, even if it was only the best of a rather poor lot, wanted Claudia and to hell with all the glass in the world. My worse wanted the tazza, preferably as well. The worst of them did not care whether I got the tazza or not so long as no one else did. That was the devil that would not let me rest. I went out to a call-box and rang Peter's number. I got no reply. I phoned his club, but they had not seen him. I wondered if David would know where he was. I pulled out a pocketful of change, checked it and asked the exchange for the Lower West Street flat. This was a temporary success for my better self.

They took a little time to find their way down to Dunstreet, and I did not in any case really expect Claudia to be at home at this hour of the evening. Then the exchange wanted my money and I put it in, and there she was on the line. She said, 'Yes? Yes? Who is it?' I thought she sounded agitated. I said, 'Claudia, it's me, Johnnie.'

'Johnnie? Where are you, then?'

'London, God help me.'

'Oh—' She did not let her breath go audibly, but there was, to my uneasy ear, measurable relief in the falling tone of the flat vowel. 'I wondered,' she said. 'You're being very expensive, Johnnie, aren't you? It's not even cheap rates yet.'

'I wanted to talk to you. No, I didn't—not consciously. As a matter of fact, I meant to telephone somebody else, but I asked the exchange for your number before I could catch myself at it. Are you all right? I thought you sounded rather distraught.'

'No. What are you doing in London?'

149

'Talking to people. Trying to talk to others, only I can't seem to find them. This afternoon I visited a charming Jewess in her incompatible maisonette at Kenton.'

'That must have been nice. What was it incompatible with?'

'Her, I think. She was a clever, civilised creature. She was old Levinson's housekeeper.'

'Levinson's housekeeper? What did you want to talk to her about?'

'Oh, you know—people and places. Who did what when. Just checking up generally.'

'I see. Let's hope your other interviews will be equally interesting.'

'They will if I can catch up with them.'

We both stopped talking. There was nothing else I wanted to say, not over the telephone. I was shaken with an almost breathless longing for the person the voice at the other end did not seem to belong to. I said, 'Claudia—'

'Yes, Johnnie?'

'I think I must come down to Dunstreet again. Is that all right?'

'All right. But tell me when. I'll be here.'

'I'll tell you.' I rang off, well inside my three minutes. But I was not at all sure, when it came to the point, that I would tell her.

I started to dial David's number and then, for the second time, changed my mind. David could not be at home yet. I did not know about Daphne. I decided to walk round there. It was a longish walk, and by the time I got there David might be just about due in.

The streets were full of the first bursts of escaping office workers, all hurrying to get ahead of the ruck. I drifted through them, feeling very timeless and detached. I was trying to reconcile in my mind my immediate need of Claudia and the hopeless intangibility of the telephone call.

I doubt if I have ever felt so ill at ease. Perhaps the home comforts of David and Daphne would have a soothing effect. At any rate, I walked steadily towards them. But I had begun to be afraid what I might be told, and I could not bear the thought of an intensified disquiet. I looked at the possibility of changing my mind once more and going and getting drunk, but a concentrated consideration of what this would feel like in practice turned me against it. I did not think it would do any good, and a booze-up is not a thing to let yourself in for unless you are pretty sure of your results. I went on walking.

It seemed a very long time before I got to David's door. There were lights inside and I thought even a smell of cooking somewhere. I rang the bell and nothing happened. After a minute or two I rang again. Then there was a bit of a flurry inside, as though someone was hoping to get to the door before whoever it was went away. Daphne opened the door. She was wearing, of all things, a dark matt housecoat zipped right up to her neck. There was a suggestion of pinkness and dampness about her, but she smelt very nice. She said, 'Johnnie! I didn't know you were in London.' She moved back from the door. 'Come in,' she said. 'I've just got out of my bath.'

I took her hand, as I sometimes did, and said, 'David back yet?' She stood there, still holding my hand, and smiled up at me. 'David's away,' she said. 'Didn't you know?'

I cannot think why, after all these years, but I bent forward suddenly and kissed her. It was still really Claudia I wanted. But I must say I was surprised at Daphne.

17

I sat in front of the fire waiting for Daphne to reappear. My head was still full of Claudia, but in a different and much less agonising sort of way. I felt separation all the time, but now my mind revolved round her as round a fixed centre, holding its distance. I was not in the least worried about David and Daphne. Daphne was a good wife, and would not let a single untoward incident affect her relations with her husband. That was in my experience the secret of good wives. It was only the nicer women who lost their hearts more than once, and they, if they did it once too often, became bad wives, which always seemed a pity. Daphne had enlarged her experience, but would step back with complete assurance into her accepted circle, gathering her skirts neatly round her. David would not suffer at all. I even wondered with a momentary amusement whether he might not, in due course, have his own experience enlarged to his greater happiness.

Daphne came out of her room and sat down opposite me. She was fully dressed now, and the effect was as severe as anything on Daphne could be. She still looked a little white and shaken, but was resolute and cheerful. At least we had no reproaches or nonsense about our never seeing each other again. I said, 'Where is David, anyway?'

'He had to go down to the country for a few days. He had—'

'Not aunt trouble, surely. Don't tell me David's developed an aunt.'

She smiled. It was interesting to see her feeling her way to a necessarily modified relation with me. The old one clearly would not do, but, as I had anticipated, she had no intention of modifying it more than decency required. The smile, regardless, still had a maternal quality. 'No, Johnnie, not really. But it is family business of a sort. He's been away several days.'

'Have you seen anything of Peter? I've tried to find him, but no one seems to know where he is.'

'Peter? No. But then we don't see all that much of him at any time.' She did not, like Mrs Larkin, actually call him that Mr Sarrett, but there was an unmistakable whiff of disapproval.

'Why do you dislike Peter?' I said.

'I don't think I dislike him. I just don't like him. There's an inhuman quality. And he's a bit mean, isn't he?'

'Over money? Not very forthcoming, I admit. I think he spends every penny he's got on the magazine.'

'But that's it, don't you see? Nothing else really interests him. I don't like these devotees. I don't think any woman does. I suspect their scale of values.'

'David says I'm potty over glass.'

'He's one to talk. Anyway, I wouldn't say you were single-minded exactly, would you, Johnnie?'

'No, indeed. Plurality is of my essence.' I gave her a warm friendly smile. I felt genuinely warm and friendly towards poor, puzzled, sedate Daphne, and all the time my mind swung in a quiet steady circle round remote Claudia. 'Anyway,' I said, 'I want to see this devotee, if I have to camp on his doorstep.'

I got up and Daphne came with me into the hall. She said, 'I do wish David would come home.'

'When do you expect him?'

'I don't know, really. He can't be away long.'

'Never mind, Daphne. David may have his aunts, but he won't come home with hairs on his coat-collar.'

She said, 'No, no, not David,' quite cheerfully, and then

153

winced almost visibly as the implications came home to her. She put a hand on my sleeve and said, 'Johnnie—'

'Don't worry, Daphne,' I said. 'Don't worry at all. A case of mistaken identity on both sides. Quite isolated.'

She cheered up again. 'All right, Johnnie. Come and see us when David is back, won't you?'

'I will,' I said, 'but not until.' We touched hands and parted. I liked Daphne better than I ever had. But I was too tired that night to look for Peter or to worry about anything much. When I did wake up, the evening, in retrospect, seemed very unlikely. But I still wanted to get hold of Peter, and there seemed to be only one way of doing that.

I rang Peter's bell at about a quarter past eight. He opened the door almost at once. He was in a dressing-gown and looked terrible. The sharp lines of his rather narrow mouth were etched in with dark, unshaved bristles. His eyes looked closer together because of the tired blackness under them. The old, sardonic quality was unimpaired. He said, 'Johnnie, what the hell are you doing up at this time of the morning?' He did not seem at all taken aback, but he made no move to ask me in.

'I tried to get hold of you several times yesterday evening, but couldn't find you. So I thought I'd catch you this morning before you went out again. Sorry if I've got you up. It's not as early as all that, in fact.'

'I know that. I was late last night. However, now that you're here, what can I do for you?'

He still stood with one hand on the door handle. I said, 'You look as if you hadn't slept for a week. Are you all right?'

'Oh yes, I'm all right. Been a bit busy—and a bit worried, to tell the truth.' I was trying to think what it was about him that looked as if he had not been to bed at all. There was no blowsiness, if that was the word I wanted. The skin looked drawn and dirty, but it was not greasy. I could not

154

see what he had on under his dressing-gown. Certainly not pyjama trousers, but he might not wear them.

'I'm sorry to worry you,' I said. 'There are one or two things I wanted to ask you.'

He said, 'Half a minute, Johnnie.' He turned and went into the sitting-room, leaving me standing where I was. I nearly went after him, but could not quite make up my mind to it. I thought I heard him moving things. Then a door shut. A moment later he came back into the hall. 'Better come in,' he said. 'I'm afraid it's all very untidy. I've cleared the worst.' There was in fact nothing visibly out of place at all. I know Peter's sitting-room fairly well. The bedroom was through a connecting door, which was shut. The place was dirty but not untidy.

Peter switched on an electric fire and said, 'I was just going to make myself some coffee. Would you like some?'

'If you're making it anyhow, yes.'

The kitchen was across the hall. He went across to it, leaving both doors open. I heard him turning on taps and clattering with tins and saucepans. I hoped he would be a long time. I had come all ready for a frontal attack, but now I was here I found it extremely difficult. I had never been much good at dealing with Peter. I could irritate him by demeaning myself, but if I tackled him on the level he could nearly always make me feel silly. I think he had that effect on a lot of people, but knowing this did not lessen the offence.

I walked to the glass-fronted book-case and looked at the twenty-three numbers of *Old Glass*. The make-up had not changed for six years, but it was still very good. Each issue had a different picture on the cover, but the spines were identical bar the serial numbers and dates. I heard Peter come back across the hall and said over my shoulder. 'How's the October number coming? It can hardly be as exciting as the last. No more news of the tazza, I suppose?'

155

'It's all right editorially. The printer's being the devil. No news of the tazza, no. Did you think there would be? Some correspondence, of course, but it's all speculative.'

'But how do you make out, Peter? I've never asked you what the printing is, but—'

'No. No, I wouldn't put it past you, but you haven't, in fact.'

'But don't tell me it pays its way.'

'I don't tell you anything, Johnnie. It's run six years, and it's the best thing of its kind. I intend to keep it so.' He went across to the kitchen again.

When he came back he said, 'There doesn't seem to be any milk. I'm very sorry. Do you mind it black?'

'Not if it's strong enough.'

'It's strong all right.'

I stirred in a good deal of sugar and sipped. It was certainly strong. I said, 'What did you gather Levinson's intentions were?'

'About what?'

'About the tazza. Had he remained in touch with the owner, or had he simply left it to the owner to make up his mind in his own time?'

'I've no means of knowing.'

'But you must have discussed it with him.'

'Only over the phone, when I had the report from him. I thought I had told you. He felt himself bound to publish, and had the owner's permission. But he had no authority to disclose the ownership, and didn't.'

'And you never heard anything more from him?'

'No. When should I have? He was dead a few days after the thing was published.'

'I didn't know whether you had seen him again before his death.'

He stood there with his back to the stove, holding his cup and saucer in front of him. What I could see of his legs looked surprisingly muscular. He was almost smiling, but his whole face was so seamed with tiredness that it was difficult to tell. His dark eyes at least were very bright, despite the rings under them. He said, 'When should I have seen him, Johnnie?'

'I don't know. I had assumed you were in touch.'

'No.' He stood there and looked at me until I got to my feet. I said, 'You look tired, Peter. You'd better get back to bed.' I made for the door.

'I'm going to. I may be seeing you, perhaps. You've been out of town, haven't you? Will you be here for a bit now?' He went to the bedroom door, put his hand on the handle and stood there. I stood in the doorway into the hall. We looked at each other across the width of the sitting-room.

'No,' I said, 'as a matter of fact I'm thinking of leaving town again this morning.'

'You're what?' He took his hand away from the door and came back a couple of paces into the room.

I said, 'I'm thinking of getting away again this morning.' The bedroom door swung slowly open behind him, and I saw the half-open suitcase and the coverlet of a made-up bed. He stared at me. Then he smiled the same smile that was half a grimace.

'You're getting to be a restless sort of chap, aren't you, Johnnie? It's time you settled down.'

'I'm thinking of it,' I said. I turned and went out into the hall. He still stood there looking at me. 'Goodbye, Peter,' I said. 'We'll meet soon, I'm sure.' I went out and shut the door behind me. I did not hear any reply.

Mrs Larkin said, 'Where have you been, then, out so early?'

'I've been to see Mr Sarrett,' I said.

'That Mr Sarrett? Don't say he was up at this time of the morning?'

'He was in his dressing-gown, anyhow. Perhaps he'd never been to bed.'

'That wouldn't surprise me. Have you had your breakfast, then?'

'Not properly. I've had some coffee.'

'And that's no good to you on an empty stomach. Sit down and I'll get you something.' I submitted to her ministrations. I was, in fact, tired with hunger and uneasiness, and I had a lot to think about.

At about ten Mrs Larkin went out to do some shopping. At a quarter past ten the phone began to ring. I let it ring until whoever it was had had enough. A little after eleven I picked up the receiver and dialled Peter's number. His phone rang busily but no one came. He might still be asleep. If he had once gone to sleep he would not, looking as he did, wake easily, and I let it ring. It must have rung for ten minutes while I sat there with the receiver resting casually on my shoulder. No one replied. Wherever Peter was, I did not think he was in bed. I put the receiver down, went into the bedroom and started to pack.

I left a note for Mrs Larkin and carried my suitcase round to the garage at the back. The first thing I saw when I opened the boot was the jemmy. The screwdriver I had allowed to become absorbed into the car tools, but I had meant to take the jemmy out. I hesitated, but Mrs Larkin might be back at any time and I did not want to get involved in explanations. It was doing no harm where it was. I flung the suitcase in on top of it and backed out.

I do not think I had any very clear idea what I was going to do in Dunstreet, but I knew I had to be there. I also knew, less explicitly but with equal certainty, that this time would settle it. I doubt if I could in fact imagine any combination of circumstances which I would accept as a completely satisfactory settlement. My mind was not working as neatly as that. There were still half-a-dozen things I wanted, pulling me this way and that and getting across each other every time I tried to think about them. I drove on, fast for me but with a curious automatic efficiency, through a countryside already turning to autumn.

I did at one point try to think myself back into the time, unbelievably recent on a calendar calculation, when neither the tazza nor Claudia had entered my field of consciousness. There they had both been, hoarding their incalculable values under the dank trees, and I had gone on living perfectly comfortably without them. The part of me that always opted for safety would have been glad to get back to that condition of unremarkable quiescence, but it was not a very important part. The subconscious may long to return to the womb, but this seldom presents itself as a feasible course of action. I did not know where I was being driven, but I was not prepared to question the forces driving me.

I passed the black car the first time when it was stopped outside a pub a bit to the west of Salisbury. It did not mean a thing to me, and I do not know why I noticed it. I must have noticed it, because when I saw it the second time I recognised it and remembered where I had seen it before. All I was conscious of then was a mild surprise that it had managed to get ahead of me, although I had not seen it pass me. This was near Swincombe, but before the Dunstreet turning. It was outside another pub. I hoped I would not meet it on the carriage-way.

I did not stop in Dunstreet at all, except for the lights. I drove straight out along the Grane road. When I came to the right-hand turn, I still did not know what I was going to do. I turned off into it, took the left fork and stopped, half under the trees. I could just see the fork in my driving mirror. It was late afternoon, dead still and heavily overcast. It was going to get dark early.

I do not know how long I sat there. I know I got

nowhere in my thinking, except that when it was dark I would walk over the bridge and along the rhododendron drive and try to see Claudia.

I heard the car change down and slither round into the side road. It was going fast, and made an astonishing racket in the breathless woods. I did not have time to get out, but saw it quite clearly in my mirror as it shot across the fork behind me. By this time it was almost embarrassingly familiar. I gave it a reasonable start. Then I backed out of the trees, manoeuvred round the tight hairpin of the fork and went after it.

18

I had never been up this road before, and I went cautiously. There was no chance in any case of my catching the lunatic ahead, but it might be possible to see where he was heading for and what he was up to.

The road ran through the crowded woods for perhaps half a mile. Then it started to climb, and a couple of minutes later the trees fell away and I saw where I was going. I should, in fact, have known before if I had stopped to work it out. Straight across the sky in front of me the long ridge ran out towards the point, and slightly left of my present course, plumb and gaunt on the skyline, the two mine workings stood up like badly worn teeth. The road, going strong for the crest of the ridge a mile or more away, looked likely to miss them by several hundred yards. But the slope was a convex one, and from where I was anything might happen to the road before it reached the top.

It was this that saved me. The slope flattened out suddenly on the shoulder of the hill, and a long stretch of dark featureless country opened up between me and the skyline. Across it, perhaps half a mile ahead of me and off to my left, the black car moved steadily away from the road and towards the nearer mine. I could not see what he was running on, and at times he disappeared altogether among the bracken and scrub thorn or behind the hummocks of the hillside. But there must be a road of some sort taking off from the tarmac and leading to the old workings. Even at this distance the surface did not look good, and the black car plunged and pitched along it at what must, to the eager man at the wheel, seem a pretty restrained pace.

I had seen quite enough. I stopped, on the upgrade, in a matter of feet and without waiting to turn backed straight down over the shoulder of the slope. Then I turned and drove down into the woods. I manoeuvred back right-handed round the hairpin, drove about to where I had stopped earlier and then, to make assurance doubly sure, ran the car well into the trees. Then I sat and waited. I do not know how long, but it was getting darker steadily all the time. If it had got much darker I should have had to choose between two alternative courses of action, which I was in no state to do. Just before this point was reached I heard what must be the black car coming hell-for-leather down the road from the top of the hill. He roared down to the Grane road, turned right with a grinding of tyres on loose metal, and made off southwards, accelerating through his gears as if he was playing squad cars.

I came out of my retreat, manoeuvred once again round the fork and drove up the hill. It was pretty dark now, but I could still just see the road, and I did not put any lights on. I nearly missed the mine turning. It did not look like a turning at all. The track was entirely grassed over, and what there was of it dipped almost at once into an abrupt hollow that might have been an old borrow-pit. It was too sudden to be natural.

I saw no point in risking my axles over the rough-riding course I had seen the black car negotiating. I stopped and left the car where it was on the track. When I switched off and got out, the silence closed in over me like deep water. The sky was battleship grey and close enough to touch, and the side of the hill buckled and threw up black uneven shapes all round me. There was nothing in between, and the track felt like a tunnel. These are not good places to walk in in the dark, but I kept my torch in my pocket until I saw the first chimney almost over me. Then I used the torch, cautiously, to see what there was to see.

Almost next to the track there was a roofless box of stone walls with nothing inside it. There was no woodwork left anywhere. The openings gaped under heavy stone lintels. I turned the torch down on to the track. Subject to my limited abilities as a tracker, which I have already pointed out, I should say that the black car had come this far and had then been backed and turned on the uneven track. If my man had gone on to the second lot of workings, he must have walked there. I could see no sign of his movements apart from the car. I went in through the near doorway. The threshold had gone, and the turf went straight in under the overhanging stone. It smelt derelict, though whatever there was to decay must have stopped decaying years ago. Brambles sprouted in two of the corners. There was nothing at all to see.

An opening on my left framed almost complete blackness. I went over to it and flashed my torch inside. It was a short tunnel roofed first with stone vaulting and then with what looked like the natural rock. Before the vaulting ended the passage was blocked completely by a heavy wooden barrier with barbed wire stapled criss-cross over it. It hugged the sides and ran up to near the roof. It was old work but still so strong that only a man using tools on the staples could have got through. This, at a point near the centre of the framing, was what someone had done.

Several strands of wire had been cast off and turned back, clearing a gap about two feet square immediately above one of the horizontal timbers. The strands had later been bent back to their original positions, but they were not fastened down. I reopened the gap, leant over the timber barrier and shone my torch forward and downwards. The tunnel ended abruptly about fifteen feet in front of me. Ahead and on both sides were vertical walls, partly of masonry and partly of natural rock. In the space between them was the head of the mineshaft. It was circular, perhaps

163

ten or twelve feet across and, except for the barrier, quite unguarded. Apart from the loose strands, all of this must have been in position any number of years. What was new was the rope. This was an inch-and-a-half hempen warp, tied securely to the bottom of the timber framing. It was obviously quite new. The end had not been whipped, but had barely started to unravel. From the foot of the barrier the rope ran across the few feet of rock floor and disappeared over the lip of the shaft. Someone had let something down the shaft. If the rope was anything to go by it was something pretty heavy. I swung a leg over the timber and climbed through the gap in the wire.

With my torch in one hand I crawled to the edge of the shaft and looked down. It was not all that deep—fifty or sixty feet, perhaps. The sides were clean and sheer, and the bottom, what my torch showed me of it, looked fairly dry. I do not know what I expected to find on the end of the rope, but certainly not what was there. It was a rope ladder, a solid affair with wooden rungs. The rope from the barrier was taken securely round the top loop just under the lip of the shaft, and the ladder hung straight down the side. It was too long for the job, and a yard or two lay loose on the floor at the bottom of the shaft. I reckoned if my man had known that, he would have brought the top of the ladder over the lip of the shaft and made it fast direct to the barrier. Perhaps he had not given himself time to think. At any rate, he had not bothered to do it. Getting started down the ladder might be a little breathless with only the warp to hold on to, but it was not dangerous.

Whatever my other mental reservations, vertigo and claustrophobia have never bothered me. Judging by the time he had been there, my man had gone down his ladder and come up again, and I had to see what he had been doing at the bottom of the shaft.

I went back to the barrier, climbed through and went

out on to the track. There was not a sound anywhere. The one thing I did not relish was the possibility of being found at the bottom of the shaft by the owner of the rope ladder, who might be sufficiently indignant at my intervention to cast it off from the top. I walked back to the car. Just visible in the windless murk, the road stretched up to the skyline and down into the tangle of trees. Nothing that I could see moved and there were no lights. I opened the boot and got the jemmy out from under my suitcase. I took it back to the mine and climbed through the barrier with it. From inside I turned the wires back into position across the gap. Then I stood the jemmy precariously on the timber bar and turned one of the wires lightly round the foot of it. If anyone started coming through, the jemmy would make enough clatter on the stone floor to give him pause and, more important, to give me warning. Once my weight was well on the ladder the warp would not be easy to cast off, and unless the man at the top was a quick thinker and carried a pretty formidable knife, I ought to be able, however lethal his intentions, to beat him to the top of the shaft. Nevertheless, I hoped he would not come.

I completed my alarm signal to my satisfaction and examined the warp and ladder until I had got the details pretty clear in my head. Then I snapped off the torch and put it in my pocket. The darkness of the uttermost pit shut in round me, but there was nothing else for it. I needed both hands and could not, at any price, risk dropping the torch. I crawled to the edge, feeling my way along the rope. When I got there, I turned round, laid hold of the rope with both hands and swung my legs over. I think it was better not being able to see. In fact the thing was not difficult. The rope was thick enough to grip without getting my hands under it and the ladder hung steady below me. I got my feet on to a rung and then, with my weight still on the rock lip, reached one hand down and took hold of the knot at

165

the top of the ladder. Without giving myself too much time
to think, I let go my other hand and swung my weight over
the edge.

For a long second I hung there, with my hands and feet
much too close together and my breath echoing on the rock
walls round me. Then I got first one foot and then the other
on to a lower rung. I no longer sagged out over the drop,
but had achieved a reasonably secure vertical. I felt with my
hands for the sides of the ladder, found them and gripped.
Then I began to go down.

There was really nothing to this at all. The only difficulty
was the natural tendency of the ladder to swing in against
the face of the shaft, but the wooden rungs held the ropes
just clear of the rock, and I could get my fingers round
them. Each time I put a foot down I kicked the slack of the
ladder out slightly and got my foot well lodged on the rung
before I let my weight carry it against the rock. I made
steady progress. There was nothing wrong with the air. It
was damp, close and quite motionless, but perfectly fresh.

The only moment of real fright was when I lowered a
foot into the bottomless blackness and came hard up against
the rock. Then, of course, it did not matter. I had reached
the bottom. I let my weight down gradually, but nothing
shifted. Still gripping the ropes against a sudden wrench,
I put the other foot down, settled it and stood. Then I took
one hand off the rope, got my torch out of my pocket and
switched it on.

The spare coils of the ladder lay about my feet. All round
me, smooth and unsensational, the sides of the shaft soared
up into invisibility. There were the openings of two galleries,
one on each side of the shaft, but both appeared to be
blocked with debris within range of the torchlight. The floor
was littered with large stone slabs. Then I saw what he
must have been up to. Against the opposite side of the
shaft, between the opening of the galleries, he had built up

166

two piles of slabs about eighteen inches apart and roofed them over with several longer slabs. It was a perfectly solid and stable structure, and provided a covered and well protected space, cube-shaped and about eighteen inches in each direction. It looked like a wall-safe designed by one of the mesolithic inhabitants of Skara Brae. A thing tucked away in there would be secure against almost anything short of earthquake. Also, unless I was mistaken, it would be quite invisible from the top, at least in any light likely to be available. The whole thing had the sort of lunatic efficiency of desperate improvisation. I took off my hat to him, but I must say he frightened me.

There was nothing else to see. I got one hand and both feet back on the bottom of the ladder, doused and pocketed the torch and began to climb. The one thing I was afraid of now was the sudden horrifying clatter of the falling jemmy, but it never came. It was strenuous but not un-endurable, and I climbed steadily until my hands found the knot at the top of the ladder. The next bit was not easy, but with that sort of thing going up is always easier than going down. I had to rely for longer than I fancied on a finger grip on the sides of the warp as it strained against the rock floor, but a moment later my weight was over the edge and I slithered forward, a little breathless but reasonably secure. I moved along the line of the rope, feeling in my pocket for the torch.

The next moment all hell was let loose, and my heart tore savagely at its moorings until sanity reasserted itself. The only thing I had not done with my alarm signal was to try it out, and I had seriously underestimated its effectiveness. I switched on the torch, recovered the jemmy from the rock floor and put it to one side against the barrier while I cleared the gap of the wires. I climbed through, put the wires back into position and walked out into the space between the roofless walls. The sky was still densely clouded, but after the shaft the night seemed almost indiscreetly bright. I put my torch away and walked unhesitatingly back along the track, making for the car.

I saw or heard nothing all the way. The excitement died out of me, and I felt suddenly an overwhelming reluctance to go on. I wanted above everything else to find Claudia, but I wanted her without complications, as I had once, but never for long, persuaded myself might be possible. It occurred to me that I must be very hungry, but I knew that this had to be accepted. The idea of driving into Dunstreet for a meal never entered my head. I backed the car in the uneven green hollow and ran it out on to the road. Then I switched the engine off and let it coast down slowly and silently to the waiting woods at the foot of the hill. Only when I was among the trees I switched on lights and engine. I drove past the fork and at the Grane road, without hesitation or calculation, turned right.

When the air began to smell salt, I turned the car off into the trees, switched off the lights and walked back to the road. I was quite close to the bridge, but in the darkness under the trees the car was safe enough. I walked down on to the bridge and stood there, leaning on the parapet and looking out over the faint phosphorescence of the water in the creek. The car on the road above was quite close before I was fully conscious of it, and I started to run only as the lights swung down the approach road to the bridge. I flung myself into the shelter of the trees as it came slowly over the bridge, and then, as the lights moved past me up the drive, knelt on the crumbling leaf mould and watched it go by. It was the green Morris with Claudia at the wheel. There was no one beside her. Her head was up and her long chin thrust slightly forward. She changed gear with easy precision as the car felt the gradient and accelerated smoothly to the bend at the top. She knew exactly where she was going.

I came out on to the drive and followed her, walking in the set rhythm of the nightmare or extreme exhaustion. When I came out among the rhododendron bushes, the back of the house was full of lights, but one after the other, as I watched, they went out.

19

When I got to the bottom of the drive I saw that the play-pen had disappeared. I suppose with Aunt Elizabeth off the active list and doctors' cars coming and going the thing was better out of the way. I stopped and for the first time made a coherent effort to take stock. I did not know what Aunt Elizabeth's condition was by now. Whether or not she was on her feet again, she might well be capable of hearing a strange voice talking to Claudia or, for that matter, strange feet on the gravel. Also, there might be other people in the house, though, knowing Coster, I did not think this likely. I must assume at least one pair each of eyes and ears and try to get in touch with Claudia in spite of them. But I was incapable of much finesse, or beyond caring.

I walked straight across to the front door. I do not think I was deliberately noisy, but I cannot remember taking any particular care to be quiet, even in that appalling silence. I put out my hand to the handle, and as I did so it moved in and away from me. Claudia was there in the hall, with one hand still on the door. The hall lights were out, but there was enough reflected light from upstairs to light me fairly adequately against the blackness behind me. The thing I remember most clearly is that for the first time she seemed to be looking up at me. Perhaps the outside step was a little above the level of the hall floor. I had not noticed it. She looked up at me from under her dark eyebrows, with her lips drawn back in a smile that showed her strong white teeth, but did not have very much welcome in it. It was only much later that I associated it with Peter's smile when

I had left him in his flat that morning. Seen from now, the two things have drawn closer together in time. When I had Claudia in front of me, the morning seemed impossibly remote, and I had already half forgotten it.

She said, 'Johnnie! When did you come?' She came outside and shut the door behind her. I do not think she ever stopped moving forward, though the time during which we looked at each other seemed consciously measurable. I must have backed away from that smile, because I had been within touch of the door, but by the time she had shut it from the outside and had her back to it we were still a couple of feet apart.

I said, 'Just now. I was by the bridge when you came in.' She still never stopped moving forward. She put a hand on my arm, and I turned and went with her. We went back across the gravel towards the bottom of the drive. When we got to the last rhododendron bush she stopped.

'You never let me know you were coming, did you, Johnnie?'

'It wasn't a deliberate decision. I came because I had to.'

'I'm sorry, Johnnie. I want you to go again. Will you please?' She had both hands on my shoulders. The fingers gripped with an unconscious desperation. Her face, tilted back only a few inches from mine, looked dead white in the darkness. 'Now, at once,' she said. 'Please, Johnnie.'

I suppose it is true that I never loved Claudia after that moment, but I loved her more then than I had ever done. I was hard driven, of course. I was tired, very hungry and frantic with an almost pathological indecision. But at that particular moment of time I was utterly in her hands. I had known almost from the beginning that this moment might come and now it had come. I had linked the fingers of my hands behind the small of her back while we stared at each other. When the door banged inside the house I felt the muscles harden as she strained backwards away from me.

171

It was startlingly loud. I had had no idea, until the noises started, how loud everything was going to be in that deadly silence. Aunt Elizabeth did not scream this time, as she had screamed over the dog, not to begin with. It was a snarling sound of almost pure rage, that boiled over gradually into frustration and panic. 'No,' she said. 'No. No. No.' She went on saying 'No' at regular but curiously long intervals, so that each time I waited consciously for the next. The words came on an ascending scale, I do not know how often, perhaps twenty times. The last time she suddenly opened her lungs and screamed at the top of her voice.

Claudia and I stood there, holding on to each other, quite rigid. I do not know whether I restrained her or whether she was, like me, in any case unable to move. Things went on happening inside the house. Lights went on and off, doors banged and there were sounds of running feet. I saw and heard them, as it were, over my shoulder but I did not move at all. I did not hear Aunt Elizabeth again after that one convulsive scream. The next identifiable noise was a car engine, which started up with a roar beyond the far end of the house. When the lights went on I saw the end of the house in silhouette against them, but they started to swing almost at once, and a moment later the car pulled out round the corner, and everything stood out in the white glare.

It was because of the glare that I saw the front door open and Aunt Elizabeth run out on to the gravel. She was wearing her red dressing-gown and felt slippers, and her hair was in two monstrous pigtails that bobbed girlishly behind her as she ran. She ran crouching forward, almost bent double, with her long arms spread wide in front of her and her little hands groping at the end of them. Her head turned this way and that, like an animal looking for something. She heard the car, of course, and I suppose she knew where

172

the end of the drive was. The lights meant nothing to her, and she ran straight into them.

The car accelerated savagely in a shower of kicked-up gravel. It was already moving fast when Aunt Elizabeth went darting across it. The near wing caught her left hand and swung her round, so that she ran, still crouching, head first into the oncoming radiator. There was a sort of crunching thud, and the great bundled body was bounced back sideways out of the track of the wheels. Then everything vanished in the blinding flare of the lights and the utter blackness that followed it. The car went up the drive without changing up again. The gears wailed like a banshee, and I could hear the tyres throwing loose metal into the bushes on both sides of the road.

I do not know how long all this took. I know that at the end of it I was still standing there and Claudia was still standing in front of me, only we no longer held on to each other. I think that was the last time I actually touched her. I took my torch out of my pocket and went over to Aunt Elizabeth. Someone had really done for her this time. Apart from the damage to the head, the neck looked pretty thoroughly broken. Claudia must have walked behind me. I found her standing opposite me, staring down at that horrible floodlit bundle. It was the broken deer in the car lamps all over again. First the deer with the dog snarling over it, then the dog with the old woman screaming over it, and now the old woman herself. There were too many dead things lying around, and I got no better at dealing with them. I do not know why it is supposed to be a good thing to know one's own weaknesses. In my experience nothing is more fatal.

Claudia put out a toe in the torchlight. She was always very elegantly shod, and I noticed now how perfect shoe and foot were. She flipped one of the off-white pigtails out of the way and studied the sideways-turned face. Then she

173

stood back from the body and looked at me. She said:

*'Let all dead things lie dead; none such
Are soft to touch.*

I do not know where she got it from, but she recited it chantingly, like an incantation. The effect was quite unbelievably horrible. Then the outside house-lights went on, and Coster appeared in the opening of the front door, calling out in a little mewing voice. 'Miss Claudia! Miss Claudia!' she said. 'Have you seen Miss Elizabeth anywhere? I thought I heard something.'

Claudia began to laugh. She stood there, feet astraddle, hands behind her back, while the laughter gradually took hold of her till the whole place rang with it. I suppose to a deaf woman it might have looked like ordinary hysteria. I stood aside and flashed my torch on what was left of Aunt Elizabeth. Coster ran over and squatted down by the body. Then she began gathering it up, but every time she got hold of some part of it something—a limb, or the lolling head, or a flap of red dressing-gown—flopped over and upset her. I expect she got it up in the end. I knew she could. I turned my back on the performance and started to walk up the drive.

I think Claudia called out after me once, but her voice was still shaken with laughter, and I did not hear it very clearly. Luckily for my emotional balance, my entire mental resources were concentrated on the business of not being sick. This struggle, walking very slowly and steadily up the slope of the drive between the rhododendron bushes, I eventually concluded to my satisfaction. I had nothing in me to be sick on, and it would have done me no good.

By the time I reached my car Claudia seemed surprisingly remote and all time at my disposal. I backed it out from under the trees and drove it steadily along the Dunstreet

road until I came to the turning left that led to the fork. I
turned left and took the right fork. When I was clear of the
trees, I pulled in to the side of the road and stopped. I did
not want to rush things, and I wished I knew how much
time had elapsed since the black car had gone whining up
the drive with its wild driver and probably a tuft of off-
white hairs on its radiator grille. I found I had very little
idea, and it did not seem worth worrying about. I drove on
up the hill without putting the lights on. This took a little
time, but I managed to find the mine track without going
past it.

The black car was parked in the first hollow. I put mine
beside it and walked on along the track. The darkness was
as dense as it had been the first time, only when I turned
into the second opening I saw, through the barrier, a shim-
mer of reflected light dancing on the darkness at the top of
the shaft. I remember thinking how disconcerting this
would have been if I had not been expecting it. I could
see, against this phosphorescence, that the gap in the barrier
had been left open, with the wires turned back. He was not
expecting visitors.

I started to climb through. I took quite a time over it,
moving with tremendous caution. I could hear noises
muffled in the shaft, and I thought sounds probably carried
both ways. I got through successfully, but must have put
one foot too far sideways. I had forgotten all about the
jemmy. I had propped it against the barrier before I
climbed out the first time and had left it there. I suppose a
man going straight to the ladder would have missed it. At
any rate, it had not been noticed. Now my foot caught it,
and it went down with the ear-splitting clatter it had made
before.

The light at the bottom of the shaft went out. I crouched
there on the warp, not moving a muscle. I breathed as

175

quietly as I could through an open mouth. I have never heard such silence.

I do not know how long this went on. Finally I put out one hand, felt the heavy cold of the jemmy and picked it up. With my other hand I eased my knife out of my pocket. I opened it with my teeth and laid it behind me with the blade resting on the warp. It was a good blade and I kept it very sharp. Then I got out my torch. With my torch in my left hand and the jemmy in my right I crawled very slowly along the line of the warp until I reached the lip of the shaft. There was still nothing from below, neither sight nor sound. I eased forward until my face was over the edge, looking down into the blackness. With my left hand I put the torch over the edge and directed it downwards. Then I waited.

It was only when I felt the first stir on the rope that I switched the torch on. The blind white face stared up at me from the bottom of the shaft, like the face of a drowned man from under the water. It was Peter all right. He had two hands on the ladder and one foot was on the lowest rung. For quite a few seconds he simply stood there, head back, staring up into the light. He did not seem very far away, despite the depth of the shaft. Then his tongue came out and flickered round his lips. 'Who's that?' he said.

'Who do you think?' I said.

We both whispered. A man left at the bottom of that shaft could have screamed his heart out, day and night, until his voice went, and nobody would have heard him, but Peter and I whispered to each other like a pair of boys in a dormitory after lights out. The shaft conducted the sounds like a speaking tube, and we had no difficulty in hearing each other.

He said, 'Johnnie!' He lifted his second foot towards the ladder.

I said, 'Stay where you are, Peter. I can cut the rope in

176

five seconds, and then you'll have to stay. Just stay where you are for the moment. I want to talk to you.'

He hung there for a moment, still with his face turned up into the light. Then once more I saw him lick his lips. He took first one foot and then the other off the ladder and stood there, still holding the ropes in his hands. He tried to smile, but it was no more warming than the last smile I had seen. He said, 'Well, Johnnie, what do you want?'

20

'You've got the tazza down there, box and all?'

'Yes.'

'Is it safe?'

'It's safe all right.' I could see Peter's cyst of stone slabs because I knew it was there. He had even got the front covered in. The thing was safe enough.

I thought for a moment, still looking down at him. 'What did old Levinson tell you? He can't have told you where the thing was.'

'He didn't. He told me the details because they were so fantastic. And he wanted me to be absolutely certain that the thing existed. I had published his report, after all. He told me about this fantastic island house buried in trees, and the blind old woman clutching her treasure and the eager up-and-coming niece. All he didn't tell me was places and names.'

'And you got those when he was dead?'

'Well—yes. I got them from you, Johnnie.'

I went back to the beginning again. I said, 'You had dinner with him the night he died?'

'Yes, I did.'

'You wanted to get money out of him, didn't you?'

'What the hell do you mean by that?'

'Don't prevaricate with me, Peter. You're not in a position to prevaricate about anything. That magazine of yours is on the rocks, isn't it?'

He tugged at the ladder with both hands, but made no other move. 'Damn you,' he said. 'Damn you, damn you,

Johnnie Slade. How I hate your guts. Only you're not worth it, really.'

'You've run out of money,' I said, 'and you thought you might raise the wind from old Levinson. But he wouldn't play. He gave you a pleasant little dinner and one of his cigars, but he told you no. Then you went off in a tizzy and he took and died.'

He shook his head suddenly. 'You've got that bit wrong,' he said. 'He died and I went off. He died right there in front of me. One moment he was talking to me and the next he put his cigar down and just stopped working.'

'That was it? And then you rooted about among his things and found what you wanted?'

'No. I told you. I got nothing from Levinson, dead or alive. The idea occurred to me, of course, just as I've no doubt it occurred to you. But you came, God damn you. I didn't know it was you, of course, not till afterwards. I heard someone ring the bell and start to come upstairs. I thought there might still be a chance to look for what I wanted, so I hid in another room on the same floor. I heard someone— you, in fact—come up and find Levinson. I hoped you would go out again and give me a chance, but after a bit I heard you telephoning, and I knew it was no use. So I got out before the crowd arrived. Only, knowing you, Johnnie, I naturally wondered what you'd been up to before you telephoned for help. And I kept an eye on you. And sooner or later what did you do? Get into your little car and drive down to Dunstreet. You brought nothing back the first time, and the second time I went after you. And what did I find at Dunstreet? A fantastic house buried in trees and a blind old woman and a more than up-and-coming niece. After that it was simply a matter of ways and means.'

'But you don't want the tazza. All you want is the money.'

'Oh, certainly. But the tazza's worth a lot of money, once the old woman's dead. How is she, by the way?'

179

'She is dead. You killed her with your car.'

For a couple of seconds there was silence. The voices—we were still whispering, God knows why—died out of that sounding tube of rock, and Peter stood there in the unwavering flood of white torchlight. This time he really smiled. He said, 'Well I'm damned. I did my best to break her bloody neck and couldn't, and then when I decide to give it up and try it the other way I go and kill her in one.'

'What do you mean, try it the other way?'

'Well—I knew where the thing was. Which, by the way, is more than you ever did, Johnnie. Anyway, I thought instead of having another go at the aunt I'd take the thing, put it away safe and then come to terms with the niece. Only now I find I have done both.'

'You were going to double-cross Claudia?'

'You could put it like that. Only trying to double-cross pretty Claudia is a bit like trying to wriggle past a rattlesnake. She's a pretty complicated piece of wickedness, Claudia.'

'She could simply go to the police.'

'Not about me, she couldn't. I know much too much. We could come to terms, all right.'

'And what are you proposing to do now, Peter? That's if I don't cut the rope.'

'You couldn't cut the rope, my dear Johnnie. I know little Johnnie. His coat is so warm, but he isn't a rope-cutter. No, we'll all have to come to terms now, won't we? You and me and our clever Claudia.' He stopped and frowned. 'You haven't told Claudia about this place, have you? You weren't so besotted as all that?'

I shook my head and then remembered that he could not see me behind the torch beam. 'No,' I said. 'No one knows about this place except you and me, Peter.' For a couple of seconds of absolute silence the implications of this sank into both of us.

Then he said, 'No, well that puts Claudia to rights anyway. The trouble with you, my poor Johnnie, is that I really believe you're not particularly interested in the money. You want the tazza. You're potty, of course. But we've always known that. I'll have to think.'

I turned the torch out, knelt back on the rock floor, put down torch and jemmy and laid hold of the warp. Then I pulled at it, hand over hand, desperately, trying to get the ladder up out of his reach. There was a scuffling at the bottom of the shaft and the rope suddenly went dead on my hands. I stood there in the darkness, breathing noisily, with the rope straining in my hands and the spare coils about my feet. Peter's voice said, 'It's no good, Johnnie.' He still whispered. 'I'm hooked on to the ladder. You can't pull me up with it, my dear Johnnie. And in any case I don't imagine you want to. You certainly can't pull it up without me.'

I threw down the warp and heard it run out again over the lip of the shaft. I knelt again and shone the torch down at him. I said, 'I must have time to think.'

He smiled quite cheerfully this time. He said, 'Do all the thinking you like, Johnnie. Only I'm coming up. I'm not staying down here while you do your thinking.'

He suddenly put one foot on the lowest rung of the ladder. He seemed quite confident. I said, 'Don't come up, Peter. My knife is here, on the rope. I can cut it in a matter of seconds. I told you. Don't come up.'

He hesitated, looking up at the torch. Then he deliberately put his other foot on the ladder and started, very slowly, to climb. He said, 'Yes, but you won't. I'm coming up, Johnnie.'

I turned, torch and all, and picked up the knife. I hacked at the uppermost strand of the rope and felt the knife bite cleanly into it. At the top of the shaft the rope crept and rolled and I could hear Peter coming breathlessly up the ladder in the darkness.

'Johnnie!' he whispered. 'Johnnie, what are you up to?

181

I'm half-way up the ladder, Johnnie. I shouldn't cut the rope now, do you think?'

I felt more fibres go under the knife edge. Then I dropped the knife and went back to the shaft. When I shone the torch down he must have been more than half-way up. He did not look more than a dozen feet below me. He came very slowly, never taking his eyes off what he knew was behind the glare of the torch. Twice more, while I watched, he moved up his hands and followed them with his feet. I said, 'Don't come any further, Peter. Can't you understand? You mustn't come any further.'

He stopped climbing and hung there. He said, 'Johnnie, Johnnie, it's no good. You can't stop me, however much you want to. And we've got to come to terms. You can't trust Claudia, you know. I know her every bit as well as you do. You know that, don't you? Better, probably.'

Something laid a very hard hand on the inside of my stomach and gripped suddenly and savagely. I let my breath out in a long sigh. Peter heard it. He said, 'To be honest, Johnnie, though of course everything is grist to her mill, I really think she prefers me. She finds you a little—well, un-orthodox, perhaps. But no hard feelings in any direction.' He began to climb again.

'Stop,' I said. 'Stop, you bloody fool.'

He shook his head. 'I'm not stopping for you, my poor old potty Johnnie. I'm coming up and we'll talk things over. You'll feel better when we've got it all straightened out and that damned thing is safe at Sotheby's.'

One rung at a time, with a rhythmical, almost hypnotic, movement which I knew was quite deliberate, Peter moved up the rope ladder until his face was no more than a couple of feet below the torch.

'No,' I said. 'No. No.' That was what Aunt Elizabeth had said, now I came to think of it. He was used to people saying no. It never seemed to make much difference to him.

I knelt up to keep the torch out of his reach, and my knee came hard up against the jemmy. I said, 'No,' again, but he smiled and moved up another rung. Quite deliberately, but quite inevitably, I laid hold of the jemmy with my right hand, balanced it and, still kneeling, swung it down in a flailing arc on the top of his head.

My torch never left his face. His expression did not change much, but he looked a bit puzzled and doubtful, as if something had gone a little wrong. A thick trickle of blood suddenly emerged from under his dark hair and ran down the side of his face and neck. It looked like a cord of red silk, pulsating gently in the torchlight. He hesitated, took one hand off the ladder and made a brushing gesture at his scalp, as if he was flicking off a fly. Then he put it back on the ladder and started to climb again. He never shielded his head even though he must have seen the second blow coming.

I had not realised quite what he would do. His expression still did not change much. His eyes were wide open, still looking at me. He simply let go of the ropes with his hands. His body turned over backwards and outwards, leaving his feet where they were. Then they came off the rung they were standing on, and he fell like a plummet, head first. The torchlight followed him all the way, and I saw the star-shaped spurt when his already damaged head hit the rock.

I stood up and tossed the jemmy down the shaft. Whatever fell down, the tazza was well protected. It made an even bigger clatter at the bottom than it had at the top, but I had suddenly seen that it did not matter how much noise I made. I snapped the torch out and put it in my pocket.

Darkness and silence closed in simultaneously, absolute darkness and absolute silence. I had not exerted myself much and was not at all out of breath. At the bottom of the shaft nothing stirred.

I had no doubts at all at this stage. I knew what I had to do. There might be some practical difficulty about getting

183

the tazza in its box up the ladder, but Peter had got it down, and there must be a bag or something. I got down on my hands and knees and crawled along the warp to the lip of the shaft.

Then I remembered the cut I had made in the top strand of the warp. I turned and crawled back to it. I looked at it closely for a moment in the light of the torch, but there was any amount of strength left.

I had been through this manoeuvre before, and there was no difficulty about it. I got both hands and feet on to the ladder and started to go down. It was in fact only when I was at least half-way down that the trouble started. That was why, in the end, I had my moments of doubt whether I was going to get up again.

I have already described the process of going down. Lower one foot, feel for the slack of the ladder, kick it clear of the rock and get the rung well under your instep before you put your weight on it. The only bad moment going down the first time had been when my exploring foot came down suddenly on rock. Now I was already half-way down when it occurred to me that it was not rock, this time, that my foot would come down on.

I stopped at once. I do not know how long for, but I must have stopped quite a time while I fought myself, hanging on that swaying ladder in the pitch darkness. If I could have had a light, or even if I had been able to persuade myself that Peter was not quite dead, it might have been possible, but I could do neither. It was that damned dog on the scullery floor, and Claudia with her horrible verses about things soft to touch.

One moment I was in doubt whether I could go on and the next I was fighting desperately to stay where I was at all. You cannot easily put your head between your knees on a rope ladder. I hooked one elbow over the rung I was holding and hung on it while the familiar waves of black

184

nausea rolled over me. It was the complaining of my arm muscles that finally roused me. Even with support for your feet you cannot hang on a rope ladder without putting a good deal of strain on the arms and shoulders.

As my head cleared, I started to climb again, and knew at once that I was going to have quite a fight to get up. I do not imagine that in fact it took me very long. It was bad at the end when I had to get my weight up over the lip of the shaft. There was only a finger grip on the warp at this stage and my hands were very tired. I pitched forward on the flat rock and lay face down for a minute or so, breathing rather noisily. Then I crawled clear of that damned shaft, took out my torch and began to untie the warp from the bottom of the barrier. It was not badly tied, but it had had quite a lot of pull on it, and there was still a dead weight dragging steadily at the bottom of the ladder. I got it undone at last and cast it off. The rope end slithered across the rock floor and whipped over the edge of the shaft like a snake going into its hole. There were plenty more rope ladders in the world.

I climbed out through the gap and put the wire strands carefully back under the retaining staples, which I hammered home with a piece of rock. Given a fresh coat of damp and grime, the whole thing would look pretty solidly undisturbed.

I walked to Peter's car. This was one of the bad moments, but the ignition key was in the lock. I put on his driving gloves, started the engine and backed the car up on to the road. I drove it down the hill and out to the end of the point. There was no beach here, but I let it bump and slither down a long slope of rock till it fetched up with its front wheels almost in the water. I left it there. I did not look for it, but there must still have been a sticky patch and a tuft of off-white hairs somewhere on the radiator grille.

Then I walked back to my car. I do not know how long this took, but there was daylight in the sky before I turned out past the signpost pointing to Grane and set course for London. Everything I did now was purely automatic, but I cannot think, looking back, that I did anything wrong.

I have not, at the time of writing, actually got the Verzelini tazza, but I know where it is, and the thing is safe enough. I shall go and get it presently. There is a card for it in my catalogue, but I have not filled in the details. I have read the books on the subject and, knowing the conditions at the bottom of the shaft, I reckon that a couple of years will be enough. The box will have rotted a bit with the damp, but not the thing itself. Come to that, almost everything rots with time, but not glass. Glass will outlast us all.

>>> If you've enjoyed this book and would like to discover more great vintage crime and thriller titles, as well as the most exciting crime and thriller authors writing today, visit: >>>

The Murder Room
Where Criminal Minds Meet

themurderroom.com